ABOUT THE TRANSLATORS

Richard Pevear has published translations of Alain, Yves Bonnefoy, Alberto Savinio, Pavel Florensky, and Henri Volohonsky, as well as two books of poetry. He has received fellowships or grants for translation from the National Endowment for the Arts, the Ingram Merrill Foundation, the Guggenheim Foundation, the National Endowment for the Humanities, and the French Ministry of Culture. Larissa Volokhonsky was born in Leningrad. She has translated works by the prominent Orthodox theologians Alexander Schmemann and John Meyendorff into Russian.

Together, Pevear and Volokhonsky have translated *Dead Souls* and *The Collected Tales* by Nikolai Gogol, *The Complete Short Novels* of Chekhov, *Anna Karenina* and *War and Peace* by Leo Tolstoy, and *The Brothers Karamazov, Crime and Punishment, Notes from Underground, Demons, The Idiot, The Adolescent,* and *The Double and The Gambler* by Fyodor Dostoevsky. They were twice awarded the PEN Book-of-the-Month Translation Prize (for their version of Dostoevsky's *The Brothers Karamazov* and for Tolstoy's *Anna Karenina*), and their translation of Dostoevsky's *Demons* was one of three nominees for the same prize. They are married and live in France.

ALSO TRANSLATED BY RICHARD PEVEAR AND LARISSA VOLOKHONSKY

THE BROTHERS KARAMAZOV *by Fyodor Dostoevsky*

CRIME AND PUNISHMENT *by Fyodor Dostoevsky*

NOTES FROM UNDERGROUND *by Fyodor Dostoevsky*

DEMONS *by Fyodor Dostoevsky*

DEAD SOULS *by Nikolai Gogol*

THE ETERNAL HUSBAND AND OTHER STORIES *by Fyodor Dostoevsky*

THE MASTER AND MARGARITA *by Mikhail Bulgakov*

THE COLLECTED TALES OF NIKOLAI GOGOL

ANNA KARENINA *by Leo Tolstoy*

WAR AND PEACE *by Leo Tolstoy*

STORIES *by Anton Chekhov*

THE COMPLETE SHORT NOVELS OF ANTON CHEKHOV

THE IDIOT *by Fyodor Dostoevsky*

THE ADOLESCENT *by Fyodor Dostoevsky*

THE DOUBLE AND THE GAMBLER *by Fyodor Dostoevsky*

THE DEATH OF IVAN ILYICH AND OTHER STORIES *by Leo Tolstoy*

DOCTOR ZHIVAGO *by Boris Pasternak*

Hadji Murat

Hadji Murat

LEO TOLSTOY

TRANSLATED FROM THE RUSSIAN BY
RICHARD PEVEAR AND LARISSA VOLOKHONSKY

WITH AN INTRODUCTION BY RICHARD PEVEAR

VINTAGE CLASSICS
Vintage Books
A Division of Random House, Inc.
New York

FIRST VINTAGE CLASSICS EDITION, OCTOBER 2012

The Cataloging-in-Publication data is available at the Library of Congress.

Vintage ISBN: 978-0-307-95134-2

www.vintagebooks.com

147028765

TABLE OF CONTENTS

INTRODUCTION

IN HIS DIARY FOR JULY 19, 1896, Tolstoy noted that, as he was crossing the fields that day, he came upon a Tartar thistle that had been broken by the plow. "It made me think of Hadji Murat. I want to write. It defends its life to the end, alone in the midst of the whole field, no matter how, it defends it." Every word here is revealing. The figure of Hadji Murat, an Avar chieftain who had fought both against and for the Russians in the Caucasus, and whom Tolstoy had first heard about in 1851 while visiting his soldier brother in Chechnya, suddenly looms up in his memory after forty-five years. Then there is the almost physical appetite of the exclamation: "I want to write." And finally, in the last passionate phrases, there is his implicit identification both with the thistle and with Hadji Murat, defending themselves "alone in the midst of the whole field." But what did Tolstoy have to defend himself against? And why "alone," when he was surrounded not only by his large family, but also by his disciples, the Tolstoyans, who came to him from Russia, Europe, America, and even, in the case of Mahatma Gandhi, from India? And how was writing his means of defense?

His novella *Hadji Murat* begins and ends with that same encounter with the Tartar thistle. It was virtually his last artistic work, and is one of his finest, if not simply *the* finest. He worked on it from 1896 to 1904, "in secret from himself," as he once confessed, because it contradicted all the aesthetic, moral, and spiritual principles he had been formulating since 1880, which had made him a world-famous public figure. It testifies, as the French translator and critic Michel Aucouturier has written, to "that which was most spontaneous and most obstinate in him," his irrepressible need for artistic creation. He would not allow it to be published during his lifetime.

But even before his encounter with the Tartar thistle, the events of 1851 had been stirring in him. On May 29, 1895, he mentioned in his diary that he was reading and enjoying the memoirs of General V. A. Poltoratsky, published in the *Historical Messenger* in 1893. Poltoratsky began his military career in the Caucasus and was a witness to some of the events described in *Hadji Murat*. Tolstoy not only drew on his memoirs in writing the book, but included him as a character. M. T. Loris-Melikov, who later became minister of the interior, also appears as a character. Tolstoy took long passages from the transcripts of his conversations with the Avar chieftain, who told him his life story. He also made use of F. K. Klugenau's journals and of his letters to Hadji Murat, and in chapter XIV he transcribed the whole of Prince M. S. Vorontsov's letter to Chernyshov, the minister of war, which he translated from the French. Documentary evidence was as important to him in writing *Hadji Murat* as it had been in writing *War and Peace*.

We see his concern with detail in a letter written as late as January 1903 to Anna Avessalomovna Karganov, the widow of the military commander of the town of Nukha (also a character in the novella), who had kept Hadji Murat in his house before his last flight:

> I turn to you, Anna Avessalomovna, with the request to answer certain questions of mine and to tell me all you remember about this man and about his escape and tragic end.
>
> Any detail about his life during his stay with you, his appearance and his relations with your family and other people, any seemingly insignificant detail which has stuck in your memory, will be very interesting and valuable to me.
>
> My questions are as follows:
>
> 1. Did he speak even a little Russian?
> 2. Whose were the horses on which he tried to escape—his own, or ones given to him? And were they good horses, and what color were they?

3. Did he limp noticeably?
4. Did the house where you lived upstairs, and he downstairs, have a garden?
5. Was he strict in observing Mohammedan rituals, the five daily prayers, etc.?

Forgive me, Anna Avessalomovna, for troubling you with such trifles, and accept my sincere gratitude for everything you do to carry out my request.

I remain, with the utmost respect, your servant,

Leo Tolstoy

P.S. Another question (6): What were the murids like who were with Hadji Murat and escaped with him, and how did they differ from him? And yet another question (7): Did they have rifles on them when they escaped?

In the same year he wrote to his cousin Alexandra, who had been a lady-in-waiting at the Russian court, asking for details about Nicholas I, though his final portrait of the emperor is far less flattering than the one she gave him.

Tolstoy likened the technique of his narrative to "the English toy called a *peepshow*—behind the glass now one thing shows itself, now another. That's how the man Hadji Murat must be shown: the husband, the fanatic . . ." (diary for March 21, 1898). Not only Hadji Murat, but all the characters and events of the novella are shown in brief flashes, taking us from the clay-walled houses of a Chechen village, to a Russian frontline fortress, to the regional capital in Tiflis, to the imperial palace in Petersburg, and back again; portraying Russians, Tartars, Cossacks, peasants, foot soldiers, officers, statesmen, Russian princesses, Tartar wives, the imam Shamil, the emperor Nicholas I. The story of the Russian peasant conscript Avdeev illustrates the technique in miniature. We are introduced to him in the second chapter; in the fifth he is badly wounded during a chance skirmish; in the seventh he dies; in the eighth Tolstoy goes back to Avdeev's native village, to his parents, family squabbles, his drunken brother, his unfaithful wife. No more is heard of Avdeev; he and his family are quite irrelevant to the main story; but like the social satire of the scenes in Tiflis and

Petersburg, like the village scenes among the Chechen mountaineers, they go to make up the world of the novella. The composition is as inclusive as in *War and Peace*, if not more so, but it is rendered with an economy of means that is the final perfection of Tolstoy's art.

The Russian Empire began expanding into the region of the northern Caucasus, peopled by the Muslim tribes of the Chechens, Ingush, and Avars, after 1783. They met with resistance almost immediately from various alliances of local forces, first under Sheikh Mansur, who called himself the "preparatory mover," and then under a series of three imams, the last of whom, Shamil, is a central figure in Tolstoy's story. Shamil, who was an Avar like Hadji Murat, maintained his opposition to the Russians from 1834 until his final surrender in 1859. Tolstoy makes him the counterpart of Nicholas I—the one with his "cold, lifeless gaze," the other "whose eyes did not look at anyone," both meting out their cruel justice.

The encounter with the Tartar thistle took Tolstoy back to his early days. As a young man in the Caucasus, he resembled the young officer Butler in *Hadji Murat*—a drinker, a gambler, a womanizer. On December 23, 1851, when he learned of Hadji Murat's coming over to the Russians, he wrote to his brother Sergei: "Hadji Murat is the leading daredevil and 'brave' in all Circassia, but he was led to commit a base action." By the time he came to write the story of that event, much had changed in the world and in himself, enough to make him see the Avar chieftain's "base action" in an entirely new way.

In 1852, Tolstoy published his first short story, "The Raid," about a Russian attack on a Chechen village. In chapter XVII of *Hadji Murat*, he returned to that same event. Few things written about the two centuries of struggle in Chechnya are as telling as the six paragraphs of this chapter, the briefest in the novella. It gives a terse, unrhetorical inventory of the results of a Russian raid on a mountain village—the same raid we have just seen in the previous chapter from Butler's jaunty point of view, the same raid Tolstoy himself took part in back in 1851. Nowhere in Tolstoy's polemical writings is there a more powerful condemnation of the senseless violence of war. Moral judgment is not pronounced in the novella; it is implicit in the sequence of events, and in the figure of Hadji Murat. He is present even where he is absent, as in the court scenes in Petersburg, or in Shamil's stronghold, or in the carousing of Russian officers in the fortress. He is the immanent measure of human dignity in this conflicted world.

Hadji Murat is a new kind of hero for Tolstoy. He is not a self-conscious seeker after the meaning of life; he is not a superior critic of a decadent society; he is not a converted sinner to whom light is revealed in extremis; he is not sensually enslaved, but also not a holy fool or an innocent. And, most unusual of all, he is not afraid of death. As a military leader, he first betrays the Chechens, then the Russians; he kills without hesitation or remorse. Yet he is neither a compromised man nor a savage: he carefully performs his ritual duties as a Muslim, he shares unquestioningly in the traditional culture of his people, and he is fiercely loyal to what is most dear to him. He is a warrior and a natural man, who, in the words of the great chorus from Sophocles's *Antigone*, finds himself "pathless on all paths." The equity of Tolstoy's portrayal of his fate lends it a transcendent beauty, set off by the indifferent singing of the nightingales. This final scene, deliberately placed out of sequence, casts its light over the whole novella, and over the whole of Tolstoy's work.

Richard Pevear

Hadji Murat

Hadji Murat

I WAS RETURNING home through the fields. It was the very middle of summer. The meadows had been mowed, and they were just about to reap the rye.

There is a delightful assortment of flowers at that time of year: red, white, pink, fragrant, fluffy clover; impudent marguerites; milk-white "love-me-love-me-nots" with bright yellow centers and a fusty, spicy stink; yellow wild rape with its honey smell; tall-standing, tulip-shaped campanulas, lilac and white; creeping vetch; neat scabious, yellow, red, pink, and lilac; plantain with its faintly pink down and faintly perceptible, pleasant smell; cornflowers, bright blue in the sun and in youth, and pale blue and reddish in the evening and when old; and the tender, almond-scented, instantly wilting flowers of the bindweed.

I had gathered a big bouquet of various flowers and was walking home, when I noticed in a ditch, in full bloom, a wonderful crimson thistle of the kind which is known among us as a "Tartar" and is carefully mowed around, and, when accidentally mowed down, is removed from the hay by the mowers, so that it will not prick their hands. I took it into my head to pick this thistle and put it in the center of the bouquet. I got down into the ditch and, having chased away a hairy bumblebee that had stuck itself into the center of the flower and sweetly and lazily fallen asleep there, I set about picking the flower. But it was very difficult: not only was the stem prickly on all sides, even through the handkerchief I had wrapped around my hand, but it was so terribly tough that I struggled with it for some five minutes, tearing the fibers one by one. When I finally tore off the flower, the stem was all ragged, and the flower no longer seemed so fresh and beautiful. Besides, in its coarseness and gaudiness it did not fit in with the delicate flowers of the bouquet. I was sorry that I had vainly destroyed and thrown away a flower that had been beautiful in its place. "But what energy and life force," I thought, remembering the effort it had cost me to tear off the flower. "How staunchly it defended itself, and how dearly it sold its life."

The way home went across a fallow, just-plowed field of black earth. I walked up a gentle slope along a dusty, black-earth road. The plowed field was a landowner's, a very large one, so that to both sides of the road and up the hill ahead nothing could be seen except the black, evenly furrowed, not yet scarified soil. The plowing had been well done; nowhere on the field was there a single plant or blade of grass to be seen—it was all black. "What a destructive, cruel being man is, how many living beings and plants he annihilates to maintain his own life," I thought, involuntarily looking for something alive amidst this dead, black field. Ahead of me, to the right of the road, I spied a little bush. When I came closer, I recognized in this bush that same "Tartar" whose flower I had vainly picked and thrown away.

The "Tartar" bush consisted of three shoots. One had been broken off, and the remainder of the branch stuck out like a cut-off arm. On each of the other two there was a flower. These flowers had once been red, but now they were black. One stem was broken and half of it hung down, with the dirty flower at the end; the other, though all covered with black dirt, still stuck up. It was clear that the whole bush had been run over by a wheel, and afterwards had straightened up and therefore stood tilted, but stood all the same. As if a piece of its flesh had been ripped away, its guts turned inside out, an arm torn off, an eye blinded. But it still stands and does not surrender to man, who has annihilated all its brothers around it.

"What energy!" I thought. "Man has conquered everything, destroyed millions of plants, but this one still does not surrender."

And I remembered an old story from the Caucasus, part of which I saw, part of which I heard from witnesses, and part of which I imagined to myself. The story, as it shaped itself in my memory and imagination, goes like this.

I

IT WAS the end of 1851.

On a cold November evening Hadji Murat rode into the hostile Chechen aoul of Makhket, filled with the fragrant smoke of kizyak.*

The strained chanting of the muezzin had just died down, and in the clear mountain air, saturated with the smell of kizyak smoke, one could hear distinctly, through the lowing of cows and the bleating of sheep dispersing among the saklyas, stuck tightly together like a honeycomb, the guttural sounds of arguing male voices and women's and children's voices coming from the spring below.

This Hadji Murat was Shamil's[1] naïb, famous for his exploits, who never rode out otherwise than with his guidon and an escort of dozens of murids caracoling around him. Now, wrapped in a bashlyk and a burka, from under which a rifle stuck out, he rode with one murid, trying to be as little noticed as possible, warily peering with his quick, black eyes into the faces of the villagers he met on the way.

Coming to the center of the aoul, Hadji Murat did not ride along the street that led to the square, but turned to the left, into a narrow lane. Riding up to the second saklya in the lane, dug into the hillside, he stopped and looked around. There was no one on the porch in front of the saklya, but on the roof, behind the freshly whitewashed clay chimney, a man lay covered with a sheepskin coat. Hadji Murat touched the man lying on the roof lightly with the handle of his whip and clucked his tongue. An old man rose from under the sheepskin coat, in a nightcap and a shiny, tattered beshmet. The old man's lashless eyes were red and moist, and he blinked in order to unstick them. Hadji Murat spoke the usual *"Salaam aleikum,"* and uncovered his face.

"Aleikum salaam," said the old man, smiling with his toothless mouth, recognizing Hadji Murat, and, getting up on his skinny legs, he started putting his feet into the wooden-heeled shoes that stood by the chimney. Once shod, he unhurriedly put his arms into the sleeves of the wrinkled, raw sheepskin coat and climbed backwards down the ladder that leaned against the roof. While dressing and climbing down, the old man kept shaking his head on its thin, wrinkled, sunburned neck and

* See glossary of Caucasian mountaineer words following text.

constantly munched his toothless gums. Having reached the ground, he hospitably took hold of the bridle and right stirrup of Hadji Murat's horse. But Hadji Murat's nimble, strong murid quickly got off his horse and, moving the old man aside, replaced him.

Hadji Murat got off his horse and, limping slightly, went up to the porch. He was met by a boy of about fifteen, who quickly came out of the door and fixed his shining eyes, black as ripe currants, on the arrivals.

"Run to the mosque, call your father," the old man ordered him, and, going ahead of Hadji Murat, he opened for him the light, creaking door of the saklya. As Hadji Murat went in, a slight, thin, middle-aged woman in a red beshmet over a yellow shirt and blue sharovary came from an inner door carrying pillows.

"Your coming bodes good fortune," she said and, bending double, she began to arrange the pillows by the front wall for the guest to sit on.

"May your sons live long," replied Hadji Murat, taking off his burka, rifle, and saber, and handing them to the old man.

The old man carefully hung the rifle and saber on nails next to the hung-up weapons of the master, between two large basins shining on the smoothly plastered and clean whitewashed wall.

Hadji Murat, straightening the pistol at his back, went to the pillows the woman had laid out and, wrapping the skirts of his cherkeska around him, sat down. The old man sat down on his bare heels facing him and, closing his eyes, raised his hands palms up. Hadji Murat did the same. Then the two of them, having recited a prayer, stroked their faces with their hands, bringing them together at the tip of the beard.

"Ne khabar?" Hadji Murat asked the old man—that is, "Any news?"

"Khabar yok"—"No news," the old man replied, looking not at the face but at the chest of Hadji Murat with his red, lifeless eyes. "I live at the apiary, I've just come today to see my son. He knows."

Hadji Murat understood that the old man did not want to tell what he knew and what Hadji Murat wanted to know, and nodding his head slightly, he asked nothing more.

"There's no good news," the old man began. "The only news is that the hares keep discussing how to drive away the eagles. And the eagles keep rending first one, then another. Last week the Russian dogs burned up the hay in Michitsky—tear their faces!" the old man croaked spitefully.

Hadji Murat's murid came in and, stepping softly over the earthen floor with the big strides of his strong legs, he took off his burka, rifle, and saber, as Hadji Murat had done, and hung them on the same nails on which Hadji Murat's weapons hung, leaving himself with only a dagger and a pistol.

"Who is he?" the old man asked Hadji Murat, pointing to the man who had come in.

"My murid. His name is Eldar," said Hadji Murat.

"Very well," said the old man, and he pointed Eldar to a place on the felt next to Hadji Murat.

Eldar sat down, crossing his legs, and silently fixed his beautiful sheep's eyes on the face of the now talkative old man. The old man was telling how their brave lads had caught two Russian soldiers the week before: they had killed one and sent the other to Shamil in Vedeno. Hadji Murat listened distractedly, glancing at the door and giving ear to the sounds outside. Steps were heard on the porch in front of the saklya, the door creaked, and the master came in.

The master of the saklya, Sado, was a man of about forty, with a small beard, a long nose, and the same black eyes, though not as shining, as the fifteen-year-old boy, his son, who ran for him and together with his father came into the saklya and sat down by the door. Having taken off his wooden shoes by the door, the master pushed his old, shabby papakha to the back of his long-unshaven head, overgrowing with black hair, and at once squatted down facing Hadji Murat.

He closed his eyes just as the old man had, raised his hands palms up, recited a prayer, wiped his face with his hands, and only then began to talk. He said there was an order from Shamil to take Hadji Murat dead or alive, that Shamil's envoys had left only yesterday, and that the people were afraid to disobey Shamil, and therefore he had to be careful.

"In my house," said Sado, "no one will do anything to my kunak while I live. But what about in the field? We must think."

Hadji Murat listened attentively and nodded his head approvingly. When Sado finished, he said:

"Very well. Now a man must be sent to the Russians with a letter. My murid will go, only he needs a guide."

"I'll send brother Bata," said Sado. "Call Bata," he turned to his son.

The boy, as if on springs, jumped up on his nimble legs and, swinging his arms, quickly left the saklya. Ten minutes later he came back with a deeply tanned, sinewy, short-legged Chechen man wearing a tattered yellow cherkeska with ragged cuffs and baggy black leggings. Hadji Murat greeted the new arrival and at once, also not wasting words, said briefly:

"Can you take my murid to the Russians?"

"It's possible," Bata said quickly, merrily. "Everything's possible. No Chechen could get through better than me. Another man would go, promise everything, and do nothing. But I can do it."

"Good," said Hadji Murat. "You'll get three for your trouble," he said, holding up three fingers.

Bata nodded his head to indicate that he understood, but added that he did not value money, but was ready to serve Hadji Murat for the honor of it. Everyone in the mountains knew Hadji Murat, how he had beaten the Russian swine . . .

"Very well," said Hadji Murat. "Rope is good when it's long, speech when it's short."

"Then I'll be silent," said Bata.

"Where the Argun bends, across from the steep bank, there is a clearing in the forest, two haystacks stand there. You know it?"

"I do."

"My three horsemen are waiting for me there," said Hadji Murat.

"Aya!" said Bata, nodding his head.

"Ask for Khan Mahoma. Khan Mahoma knows what to do and what to say. Take him to the Russian chief, to Vorontsov, the prince.[2] Can you do that?"

"I'll take him."

"Take him and bring him back. Can you do that?"

"I can."

"Take him, and return with him to the forest. I will be there, too."

"I will do it all," Bata said, stood up and, putting his hands to his chest, went out.

"Another man must be sent to Gekhi," said Hadji Murat, when Bata had gone. "In Gekhi here is what must be done," he began, taking hold of one of the cartridge bands on his cherkeska, but he dropped his hand at once and fell silent, seeing two women come into the saklya.

One was Sado's wife, the same thin, middle-aged woman who had arranged the pillows. The other was a very young girl in red sharovary and a green beshmet, with a curtain of silver coins covering her whole breast. At the end of her black braid, not long but stiff, thick, which lay between the shoulder blades on her thin back, hung a silver rouble; the same black-currant eyes as her father and brother shone merrily on her young face, which was trying to look stern. She did not glance at the guests, but was obviously aware of their presence.

Sado's wife carried a low, round table on which there were tea, dumplings, pancakes with butter, cheese, churek—a thinly rolled-out bread—and honey. The girl carried a basin, a kumgan, and a towel.

Sado and Hadji Murat were silent all the while the women, moving quietly in their soleless red chuviaki, were setting what they had brought before the guests. Eldar, his sheep's eyes directed at his crossed legs, was immobile as a statue all the while the women were in the saklya. Only when they left and their soft steps had died away completely behind the door, did Eldar sigh with relief and Hadji Murat take out one of the cartridges of his cherkeska, remove the bullet that stopped it up, and, from under the bullet, a note rolled into a tube.

"To my son," he said, pointing to the note.

"Where to reply?" asked Sado.

"To you, and you deliver it to me."

"It will be done," said Sado, and he put the note into a cartridge of his cherkeska. Then, taking the kumgan, he moved the basin towards Hadji Murat. Hadji Murat rolled up the sleeves of his beshmet on his muscular arms, white above the hands, and held them under the stream of cold, transparent water that Sado was pouring from the kumgan. Having wiped his hands on a clean, rough towel, Hadji Murat turned to the food. Eldar did the same. While the guests were eating, Sado sat facing them and thanked them several times for coming. The boy, sitting by the door, not taking his shining black eyes from Hadji Murat, was smiling, as if to confirm his father's words by his smile.

Though Hadji Murat had eaten nothing for more than twenty-four hours, he ate only a little bread and cheese, and, taking a small knife from under his dagger, gathered up some honey and spread it on bread.

"Our honey is good. This year of all years the honey is both plentiful and good," said the old man, obviously pleased that Hadji Murat was eating his honey.

"Thank you," said Hadji Murat and drew back from the food.

Eldar would have liked to eat more, but, like his murshid, he moved away from the table and gave Hadji Murat the basin and the kumgan.

Sado knew that in receiving Hadji Murat he was risking his life, because after the quarrel between Shamil and Hadji Murat, it had been announced to all the inhabitants of Chechnya that, on pain of death, they were not to receive Hadji Murat. He knew that the inhabitants of the aoul might learn of Hadji Murat's presence at any moment and might demand that he be handed over. But that not only did not trouble Sado, it even gladdened him. Sado considered it his duty to defend his guest—his kunak—even if it cost him his life, and he was glad in himself and proud of himself that he was acting as one should.

"While you are in my house and my head is on my shoulders, no one will do anything to you," he repeated to Hadji Murat.

Hadji Murat looked attentively into his shining eyes and, understanding that this was true, said with a certain solemnity:

"May you be granted joy and life."

Sado silently pressed his hand to his chest in a sign of gratitude for the kind words.

Having closed the shutters of the saklya and kindled the wood in the fireplace, Sado, in a particularly merry and excited state, left the guest room and went to the part of the saklya where his whole family lived. The women were not asleep yet and were talking about the dangerous guests who were spending the night in their guest room.

II

THAT SAME NIGHT, at the frontier fortress of Vozdvizhenskoe, some ten miles from the aoul where Hadji Murat was spending the night, three soldiers and a corporal left the stronghold by the Chakhgirinsky gate. The soldiers were wearing sheepskin jackets and papakhas, with rolled-up greatcoats on their shoulders, and big boots above the knee, as soldiers in the Caucasus went around then. The soldiers, with muskets on their shoulders, first went along the road, then, having gone some five hundred paces, turned off and, their boots rustling over dry leaves, went some twenty paces to the right and stopped by a broken chinara, whose black trunk was visible even in the darkness. The listening post was usually sent to this chinara.

The bright stars that had seemed to race over the treetops while the soldiers walked through the forest now stopped, shining brightly between the bare branches of the trees.

"It's dry—thanks be for that," said Corporal Panov, taking his long musket with its bayonet from his shoulder and leaning it with a clank against the trunk of a tree. The three soldiers did the same.

"That's it—I've lost it," Panov grumbled crossly. "Either I forgot it, or it fell out on the way."

"What are you looking for?" asked one of the soldiers in a lively, cheerful voice.

"My pipe. Devil knows what's become of it!"

"Is the stem still there?" asked the lively voice.

"Yes, here it is."

"Then why not right in the ground?"

"Ah, come on."

"I'll set it up in a flash."

Smoking at a listening post was forbidden, but this was not really a listening post, but more of an advance patrol, which was sent out so that the mountaineers could not bring a cannon up surreptitiously, as they used to do, and fire at the stronghold, and Panov did not consider it necessary to deprive himself of smoking and therefore agreed to the cheerful soldier's suggestion. The cheerful soldier took a knife from his pocket and began digging in the ground. Having dug out a little hole, he smoothed it all around, pressed the pipe stem into it, then filled the hole with tobacco, tamped it down, and the pipe was ready. The sulfur match flame lit up for a moment the high-cheekboned face of the soldier lying on his belly. There was a whistling in the stem, and Panov caught the pleasant smell of burning shag.

"All set up?" he said, getting to his feet.

"That it is."

"Fine lad you are, Avdeev! A foxy fellow. Well, then?"

Avdeev rolled aside, giving his place to Panov and letting smoke out of his mouth.

Having had their smoke, the soldiers started a conversation among themselves.

"They say the company commander got into the cash box again. Seems he lost at cards," one of the soldiers said in a lazy voice.

"He'll pay it back," said Panov.

"Sure, he's a good officer," Avdeev confirmed.

"Good, yes, good," the one who had started the conversation went on gloomily, "but my advice is that the company should have a talk with him: if you've taken, tell us how much, and when you'll pay it back."

"That's as the company decides," said Panov, tearing himself away from the pipe.

"Sure thing—we're all one big man," Avdeev agreed.

"We've got to buy oats and get boots by spring, we need cash, and if he's taken it . . ." the disgruntled man insisted.

"I said, it's as the company wants," repeated Panov. "It's not the first time: he takes and pays it back."

At that time in the Caucasus every company administered all its practical affairs through its own chosen people. They received cash from the treasury to the amount of six roubles fifty kopecks per man and supported themselves on it: planted cabbage, made hay, kept their own carts, pranced about on well-fed company horses. The company money was kept in a cash box, the key to which was kept by the company commander, and it often happened that the company commander borrowed from the company cash box. So it was now, and it was this that the soldiers were talking about. The gloomy soldier Nikitin wanted to demand an accounting from the commander, but Panov and Avdeev considered that there was no need for that.

After Panov, Nikitin also had a smoke and, spreading his greatcoat under him, sat leaning against a tree. The soldiers quieted down. Only the wind could be heard rustling in the treetops high above their heads. Suddenly the howling, shrieking, wailing, and laughing of jackals came through that ceaseless, quiet rustling.

"Hear how the cursed things pour it out!" said Avdeev.

"It's you they're laughing at, because your mug's all askew," said the high Ukrainian voice of the fourth soldier.

Again everything was quiet, only the wind rustled in the branches, now covering, now uncovering the stars.

"Say, Antonych," the cheerful Avdeev suddenly asked Panov, "do you ever feel heartsick?"

"What do you mean, heartsick?" Panov answered reluctantly.

"I sometimes feel so heartsick, so heartsick, it's like I don't know what I may do to myself."

"Ah, you!" said Panov.

"That time when I drank up the money, it was all from feeling heartsick. It came over me, just came over me. I thought: why don't I get crocked?"

"Drink can make it worse."

"And did. But how can you get away from it?"

"What are you heartsick for?"

"Me? For home."

"So, it was a rich life there?"

"Not rich, but a right life. A good life."

And Avdeev started telling what he had already told many times to the same Panov.

"I volunteered to go for my brother," Avdeev told them. "He had four children! And they'd only just married me off. Mother started pleading. I think: what's it to me? Maybe they'll remember my kindness. I went to the master. Our master was nice, he said: 'Good boy! Off you go!' And so I went for my brother."

"Well, that's a good thing," said Panov.

"But would you believe it, Antonych, I'm heartsick now. And I'm heartsick most of all because, I say, why did you go for your brother? He lives like a king now, I say, and you suffer. And the more I think, the worse it gets. Some kind of sin, surely."

Avdeev fell silent.

"Maybe we'll have another smoke?" asked Avdeev.

"Well, set it up, then!"

But the soldiers were not to have their smoke. Avdeev had just stood up and begun setting up the pipe, when they heard through the rustling of the wind the sound of footsteps coming down the road. Panov took his musket and shoved Nikitin with his foot. Nikitin got to his feet and picked up his greatcoat. The third man—Bondarenko—also stood up.

"And I had such a dream, brothers . . ."

Avdeev hissed at Bondarenko, and the soldiers froze, listening. The soft footsteps of people not shod in boots were coming near. The crunch of twigs and dry leaves could be heard more and more clearly in the darkness. Then talk was heard in that special guttural tongue spoken by the Chechens. The soldiers now not only heard but saw two shadows passing in the spaces between the trees. One shadow was shorter, the other taller. When the shadows came even with the soldiers, Panov, gun in hand, stepped out on the road with two of his comrades.

"Who goes there?" he called out.

"Peaceful Chechen," said the shorter one. It was Bata. "Gun *yok*, saber *yok*," he said, pointing to himself. "Want preenze."

The taller one stood silently beside his comrade. He also wore no weapons.

"An emissary. That means—to the regimental commander," Panov said, explaining to his comrades.

"Much want Preenze Vorontsov, want big business," said Bata.

"All right, all right, we'll take you," said Panov. "Well, so take them, you and Bondarenko," he turned to Avdeev, "and once you've handed them over to the officer of the day, come back. Watch out," said Panov, "be careful, tell them to walk ahead of you. These shave-heads can be tricky."

"And what about this?" said Avdeev, making a stabbing movement with his bayonet. "One little poke, and he's out of steam."

"What's he good for if you stab him?" said Bondarenko. "Well, off with you!"

When the footsteps of the two soldiers and the emissaries died away, Panov and Nikitin went back to their place.

"Why the devil do they go around at night!" said Nikitin.

"Must mean they've got to," said Panov. "It's turning chilly," he added and, unrolling his greatcoat, he put it on and sat down by the tree.

About two hours later Avdeev and Bondarenko came back.

"So you handed them over?" asked Panov.

"Yes. They're not asleep yet at the regimental commander's. We took them straight to him. And what nice lads these shave-heads are," Avdeev went on. "By God! I got to talking with them."

"You'd be sure to," Nikitin said with displeasure.

"Really, they're just like Russians. One's married. *'Marushka bar?'* I say. *'Bar,'* he says. *'Baranchuk bar?'* I say. *'Bar.'* 'Many?' 'A couple,' he says. Such a nice talk we had! Nice lads."

"Nice, yes," said Nikitin, "just meet him face-to-face, he'll spill your guts for you."

"Should be dawn soon," said Panov.

"Yes, the stars are already going out," said Avdeev, sitting down.

And the soldiers became quiet again.

III

THE WINDOWS of the barracks and the soldiers' houses had long been dark, but in one of the best houses of the fortress the windows were all still lit up. This house was occupied by the commander of the Kurinsky regiment, the son of the commander in chief, the imperial adjutant Prince Semyon Mikhailovich Vorontsov. Vorontsov lived with his wife, Marya Vassilievna, a famous Petersburg beauty, and lived in such luxury in the small Caucasian fortress as no one had ever lived there before. To Vorontsov, and especially to his wife, it seemed that they lived not only a modest life, but one filled with privation; but this life astonished the local people by its extraordinary luxury.

Now, at twelve midnight, in a large drawing room with a wall-to-wall carpet, with the heavy curtains drawn, at a card table lighted by four candles, the host and hostess sat with their guests and played cards. One of the players was the host himself, a long-faced, fair-haired colonel with an imperial adjutant's insignia and aglets, Vorontsov; his partner was a graduate of Petersburg University, a disheveled young man of sullen appearance, recently invited by Princess Vorontsov as a tutor for her little son by her first marriage. Against them played two officers: one the broad-faced, red-cheeked company commander, Poltoratsky,[3] transferred from the guards; the other a regimental adjutant, who sat very straight, with a cold expression on his handsome face. Princess Marya Vassilievna herself, an ample, big-eyed, dark-browed beauty, sat next to Poltoratsky, touching his legs with her crinoline and peeking at his cards. In her words, and in her glances, and in her smile, and in all the movements of her body, and in the scent that wafted from her, there was something that drove Poltoratsky to obliviousness of everything except the awareness of her proximity, and he made mistake after mistake, annoying his partner more and more.

"No, this is impossible! You've squandered your ace again!" said the adjutant, turning all red, when Poltoratsky discarded an ace.

Poltoratsky, as if waking up, gazed without understanding at the displeased adjutant with his kind, wide-set, dark eyes.

"Well, forgive him!" Marya Vassilievna said, smiling. "You see, I told you," she said to Poltoratsky.

"But you said something else entirely," Poltoratsky said, smiling.

"Did I really?" she said and also smiled. And this returned smile flustered and delighted Poltoratsky so terribly that he turned a deep red and, seizing the cards, began to shuffle them.

"It's not your turn to shuffle," the adjutant said sternly, and his white hand with its signet ring began dealing the cards as if he only wanted to get rid of them as quickly as possible.

The prince's valet came into the drawing room and announced that the officer of the day was asking to see the prince.

"Excuse me, gentlemen," Vorontsov said, speaking Russian with an English accent. "Will you sit in for me, Marie?"

"Do you agree?" the princess asked, quickly and lightly rising to her full, tall height, rustling her silks, and smiling her radiant smile of a happy woman.

"I always agree to everything," said the adjutant, very pleased that the princess, who was quite unable to play, would now be playing against him. Poltoratsky only spread his arms, smiling.

The rubber was nearing its end when the prince returned to the drawing room. He was especially cheerful and excited.

"Do you know what I propose?"

"Well?"

"That we drink some champagne."

"I'm always ready for that," said Poltoratsky.

"Say, that's a very nice idea," said the adjutant.

"Serve it, Vassily!" said the prince.

"Why did they send for you?" asked Marya Vassilievna.

"It was the officer of the day and another man."

"Who? For what?" Marya Vassilievna asked hastily.

"I can't tell you," said Vorontsov, shrugging his shoulders.

"Can't tell me?" Marya Vassilievna repeated. "We'll see about that."

Champagne was brought. The guests drank a glass and, having finished the game and settled accounts, began taking their leave.

"Is it your company that's assigned to the forest tomorrow?" the prince asked Poltoratsky.

"Yes, mine. Why?"

"Then we'll see each other tomorrow," said the prince, smiling slightly.

"Very glad," said Poltoratsky, without quite understanding what Vorontsov was telling him and preoccupied only with the fact that he was about to press Marya Vassilievna's big white hand.

Marya Vassilievna, as always, not only pressed Poltoratsky's hand firmly but even shook it hard. And, reminding him once more of his mistake in leading diamonds, she smiled at him, as it seemed to Poltoratsky, with a lovely, tender, and significant smile.

POLTORATSKY WENT HOME in that rapturous state which can be understood only by people like himself, who grew up and were educated in society, when, after months of isolated military life, they again meet a woman from their former circle. And, moreover, such a woman as Princess Vorontsov.

On reaching the little house where he lived with a comrade, he pushed the front door, but it was locked. He knocked. The door did not open. He became vexed and started beating on the locked door with his foot and his saber. Footsteps were heard behind the door, and Vavilo, Poltoratsky's domestic serf, lifted the hook.

"What made you think of locking it!? Blockhead!"

"Ah, how can you, Alexei Vladimir. . ."

"Drunk again! I'll show you how I can . . ."

Poltoratsky was about to hit Vavilo, but changed his mind.

"Well, devil take you. Light a candle."

"This minute."

Vavilo was indeed tipsy, and he had been drinking because he had been to a name-day party at the quartermaster's. On coming home, he fell to thinking about his life in comparison with the life of Ivan Makeich, the quartermaster. Ivan Makeich had income, was married, and hoped for a full discharge in a year. As a boy, Vavilo had been "taken upstairs," that is, to wait on his masters, and now he was already past forty, but was still not married and lived a campaign life with his desultory master. He was a good master, beat him little, but what sort of life was it! "He's promised to give me my freedom when he returns from the Caucasus. But where am I to go with my freedom? It's a dog's life!" thought Vavilo. And he became so sleepy that, fearing lest someone come in and steal something, he hooked the door and fell asleep.

Poltoratsky went into the room where he slept with his comrade Tikhonov.

"Well, what, did you lose?" said Tikhonov, waking up.

"Oh, no, I won seventeen roubles, and we drank a bottle of Cliquot."

"And looked at Marya Vassilievna?"

"And looked at Marya Vassilievna," Poltoratsky repeated.

"It'll be time to get up soon," said Tikhonov, "and we must set out at six."

"Vavilo," cried Poltoratsky. "See that you wake me up properly at five in the morning."

"How can I wake you up if you hit me?"

"I said wake me up. Do you hear?"

"Yes, sir."

Vavilo left, taking away the boots and clothes.

And Poltoratsky got into bed and, smiling, lit a cigarette and put out the candle. In the darkness he saw before him the smiling face of Marya Vassilievna.

AT THE VORONTSOVS' they also did not go to asleep at once. When the guests left, Marya Vassilievna went up to her husband and, standing in front of him, said sternly:

"Eh bien, vous allez me dire ce que c'est?"

"Mais, ma chère . . ."

"Pas de 'ma chère'! C'est un émissaire, n'est-ce pas?"

"Quand même je ne puis pas vous le dire."

"Vous ne pouvez pas? Alors c'est moi qui vais vous le dire!"

*"Vous?"**

"Hadji Murat? Yes?" said the princess, who had been hearing for several days already about the negotiations with Hadji Murat and supposed that Hadji Murat himself had come to see her husband.

Vorontsov could not deny it, but disappointed his wife in that it was not Hadji Murat himself, but only his emissary, who had announced that Hadji Murat would come over to him the next day at the place appointed for woodcutting.

* "Well, are you going to tell me what it is?"
"But, my dear . . ."
"No 'my dear'! It's an emissary, isn't it?"
"Even so I can't tell you."
"You can't? Then it's I who will tell you!"
"You?"

Amidst the monotony of their life in the fortress, the Vorontsovs—husband and wife—were very glad of this event. Having talked about how pleased his father would be with this news, the husband and wife went to bed past two o'clock.

IV

After the three sleepless nights he had spent fleeing from the murids Shamil sent against him, Hadji Murat fell asleep as soon as Sado left the saklya, wishing him a good night. He slept without undressing, his head resting on his arm, the elbow sunk deep in the red down pillows his host had laid out for him. Not far from him, near the wall, slept Eldar. Eldar lay on his back, his strong young limbs spread wide, so that his high chest, with black cartridges on a white cherkeska, was higher than his freshly shaven blue head thrown back and fallen from the pillow. Pouting slightly like a child's, his upper lip, barely covered with down, contracted and then relaxed as if sipping something. He slept as did Hadji Murat: dressed, with a pistol and dagger in his belt. In the fireplace of the saklya, the logs were burning down, and a night lamp shone faintly from a niche in the small stove.

In the middle of the night the door of the guest room creaked, and Hadji Murat instantly sat up and put his hand to his pistol. Sado came into the room, stepping softly over the earthen floor.

"What is it?" Hadji Murat asked briskly, as if he had never been asleep.

"We must think," said Sado, squatting in front of Hadji Murat. "A woman on the roof saw you ride in," he said, "and told her husband, and now the whole aoul knows. A neighbor just ran by and told my wife that the old men have gathered by the mosque and want to detain you."

"We must go," said Hadji Murat.

"The horses are ready," Sado said and quickly left the room.

"Eldar," Hadji Murat whispered, and Eldar, hearing his name and, above all, the voice of his murshid, jumped up on his strong legs, straightening his papakha. Hadji Murat put on his weapons over his burka. Eldar did the same. And the two men silently went out of the saklya onto the porch. The black-eyed boy brought the horses. At the clatter of hoofs on the beaten earth of the street, some head stuck out the door of a neighboring saklya, and, with a clatter of wooden shoes, someone went running up the hill towards the mosque.

There was no moon, but the stars shone brightly in the black sky, and the outlines of the roofs of saklyas could be seen in the darkness and, larger than the others, the edifice of the mosque with its minaret in the upper part of the aoul. A hum of voices came from the mosque.

Hadji Murat, quickly seizing his gun, put his foot into the narrow stirrup and, noiselessly, inconspicuously throwing his body over, inaudibly seated himself on the high cushion of the saddle.

"May God reward you!" he said, addressing his host, feeling for the other stirrup with a habitual movement of the right foot, and he lightly touched the boy who was holding the horse with his whip, as a sign that he should step aside. The boy stepped aside, and the horse, as if knowing himself what had to be done, set off at a brisk pace down the lane towards the main road. Eldar rode behind; Sado, in a fur coat, swinging his arms rapidly, almost ran after them, crossing from one side of the narrow street to the other. At the end, across the road, a moving shadow appeared, then another.

"Stop! Who goes there? Halt!" a voice cried, and several men barred the road.

Instead of stopping, Hadji Murat snatched the pistol from his belt and, putting on speed, aimed his horse straight at the men barring the road. The men standing in the road parted, and Hadji Murat, without looking back, set off down the road at a long amble. Eldar followed him at a long trot. Behind them two shots cracked, two bullets whistled by, hitting neither him nor Eldar. Hadji Murat went on riding at the same pace. Having gone some three hundred paces, he stopped the slightly panting horse and began to listen. Ahead, below, was the noise of swift water. Behind, in the aoul, came the roll call of the cocks. Above these sounds, voices and the tramp of approaching horses could be heard from behind Hadji Murat. Hadji Murat touched up his horse and rode on at the same steady pace.

Those riding behind galloped and soon caught up with Hadji Murat. They were some twenty mounted men. They were inhabitants of the aoul, who had decided to detain Hadji Murat, or at least to pretend that they wanted to detain him, so as to clear themselves before Shamil. When they came close enough to be seen in the darkness, Hadji Murat stopped, dropped the reins, and, unbuttoning the cover of his rifle with an accustomed movement of his left hand, drew it out with his right. Eldar did the same.

"What do you want?" cried Hadji Murat. "To take me? So, take me!" and he raised his rifle. The inhabitants of the aoul stopped.

Hadji Murat, holding the rifle in his hand, began to descend into the hollow. The riders, without coming closer, went after him. When Hadji Murat crossed to the other side of the hollow, the mounted men following him called out that he should listen to what they wanted to say. In response to that, Hadji Murat fired his rifle and sent his horse into a gallop. When he stopped, the pursuit behind him could no longer be heard; nor could the cocks be heard; only the murmur of water could be heard more clearly in the forest, and the occasional lament of an owl. The black wall of the forest was quite close. This was the same forest where his murids were waiting for him. Having ridden up close to it, Hadji Murat stopped and, drawing a quantity of air into his lungs, whistled and then fell silent, listening. After a moment, the same whistle was heard from the forest. Hadji Murat turned off the road and went into the forest. Having gone about a hundred paces, Hadji Murat saw a campfire between the trunks of the trees, the shadows of men sitting by it, and, half lit by the fire, a hobbled horse with a saddle.

One of the men sitting by the fire rose quickly and went to Hadji Murat, taking hold of his bridle and stirrup. It was the Avar[4] Hanefi, Hadji Murat's adopted brother, who managed his household.

"Put out the fire," said Hadji Murat, getting off his horse. The men started scattering the campfire and stamping on the burning branches.

"Was Bata here?" asked Hadji Murat, going over to the spread-out burka.

"He was. He left long ago with Khan Mahoma."

"What road did they take?"

"That one," replied Hanefi, pointing the opposite way from that by which Hadji Murat had come.

"All right," said Hadji Murat and, taking off his rifle, he began to load it. "We must be careful, they pursued me," he said, addressing the man who was putting out the fire.

This was the Chechen Gamzalo. Gamzalo went to the burka, picked up a rifle lying there in its cover, and silently went to the edge of the clearing, to the place Hadji Murat had come from. Eldar, getting off his horse, took Hadji Murat's horse and, pulling the heads of both up high, tied them to trees, then, like Gamzalo, stood at the other edge of the clearing, his rifle behind his shoulders. The campfire was extinguished, and the forest no longer seemed as dark as before, and stars still shone, though faintly, in the sky.

Looking at the stars, at the Pleiades already risen halfway up the sky, Hadji Murat calculated that it was already long past midnight and that it had long been time for the night's prayer. He asked Hanefi for the kumgan that they always carried with them in their baggage, and, putting on his burka, went towards the water.

After taking off his shoes and performing the ablution, Hadji Murat stood barefoot on the burka, then squatted on his calves and, first stopping his ears with his fingers and closing his eyes, turned to the east and said his usual prayers.

Having finished his prayers, he went back to his place, where his saddlebags were, and, sitting on his burka, rested his hands on his knees, bowed his head, and fell to pondering.

Hadji Murat had always believed in his luck. When he undertook something, he was firmly convinced beforehand of success—and everything succeeded for him. That had been so, with rare exceptions, in the whole course of his stormy military life. So he hoped it would be now as well. He imagined himself, with the army Vorontsov would give him, going against Shamil and taking him prisoner, and avenging himself, and how the Russian tsar would reward him, and he again would rule not only Avaria, but also the whole of Chechnya, which would submit to him. With these thoughts he did not notice how he fell asleep.

He dreamed of how he and his brave men, singing and shouting "Hadji Murat is coming," swoop down on Shamil and take him and his wives, and hear his wives weeping and wailing. He woke up. The song "*La ilaha,*"[5] and the shouts of "Hadji Murat is coming," and the weeping of Shamil's wives—these were the howling, weeping, and laughter of the jackals, which woke him up. Hadji Murat raised his head, looked through the tree trunks at the sky already brightening in the east, and asked the murid sitting some distance from him about Khan Mahoma. Learning that Khan Mahoma had not come back yet, Hadji Murat lowered his head and at once dozed off again.

He was awakened by the merry voice of Khan Mahoma, coming back with Bata from his embassy. Khan Mahoma sat down at once by Hadji Murat and began telling about how the soldiers had met them and taken them to the prince himself, how the prince was glad and promised to meet them tomorrow where the Russians would be cutting wood, across the Michik, at the Shalinskoe clearing. Bata interrupted his comrade's speech, putting in his own details.

Hadji Murat asked in detail about the precise words in which Vorontsov had responded to the proposal of Hadji Murat going over to the Russians. And Khan Mahoma and Bata said with one voice that the prince had promised to receive Hadji Murat as his guest and make it so that all would be well for him. Hadji Murat also asked about the road, and when Khan Mahoma assured him that he knew the road well and would bring him straight there, Hadji Murat took out some money and gave Bata the promised three roubles; and he told his own men to take his gold-inlaid arms and the papakha with a turban from the saddlebags, and to clean themselves up, so as to come to the Russians looking well. While the weapons, saddles, bridles, and horses were being cleaned, the stars grew pale, it became quite light, and a predawn breeze sprang up.

V

Early in the morning, while it was still dark, two companies with axes, under the command of Poltoratsky, went out seven miles from the Chakhgirinsky gate and, posting a line of riflemen, set about cutting wood as soon as it became light. By eight o'clock the mist, which had merged with the fragrant smoke of damp branches hissing and crackling on the bonfires, began to lift, and the woodcutters, who earlier, from five paces away, could not see but could only hear each other, began to see both the bonfires and the forest road choked with trees; the sun now appeared as a bright spot in the mist, now disappeared again. In a small clearing off the road, Poltoratsky, his subaltern Tikhonov, two officers of the third company, and Poltoratsky's comrade from the Corps of Pages, Baron Freze, a former horse guard demoted to the ranks for dueling, were sitting on drums. Around the drums lay food wrappings, cigarette butts, and empty bottles. The officers had drunk vodka, eaten a bit, and were drinking porter. The drummer was uncorking the eighth bottle.

Poltoratsky, though he had not had enough sleep, was in that special state of high spirits and kindly, carefree merriment, which he always felt among his soldiers and comrades where there might be danger.

The officers were having a lively conversation about the latest news, the death of General Sleptsov. No one saw in that death the most important moment of that life—its ending and returning to the source from which it had come—but saw only the gallantry of a dashing officer falling upon the mountaineers with his saber and desperately cutting them down.

Though everyone, especially officers who had been in action, could and did know that neither in the war then in the Caucasus nor anywhere else could there ever be that hand-to-hand cutting down with sabers which is always surmised and described (and if there is such hand-to-hand combat with sabers and bayonets, it is only those running away who are cut down and stabbed), this fiction of hand-to-hand combat was recognized by the officers and lent them that calm pride and gaiety with which they were sitting on the drums, some in dashing, others, on the contrary, in the most modest poses, smoking, drinking, and joking, not troubling about death, which, as it had Sleptsov, might overtake each of them at any moment. And indeed, as if to confirm their expectations, in the midst of their talk they heard, to the left of the road, the bracing, beautiful sound of a sharp, cracking rifle shot, and with a merry whistle a little bullet flew by somewhere in the foggy air and smacked into a tree. A few ponderously loud booms of the soldiers' muskets answered the enemy shot.

"Aha!" Poltoratsky cried in a merry voice, "that's from the line! Well, brother Kostya," he turned to Freze, "here's your chance. Go to your company. We'll arrange a lovely battle for them! And put you up for a promotion."

The demoted baron jumped to his feet and went at a quick pace to the smoky area where his company was. A small, dark bay Kabarda horse was brought to Poltoratsky, he mounted it, and, forming up his company, led it towards the line in the direction of the shooting. The line stood at the edge of the forest before the bare slope of a gully. The wind was blowing towards the forest, and not only the slope, but the far side of the gully was clearly visible.

As Poltoratsky rode up to the line, the sun emerged from the fog, and on the opposite side of the gully, by the sparse young forest that began there, some two hundred yards away, several horsemen could be seen. These Chechens were the ones who had pursued Hadji Murat and wanted to see his coming to the Russians. One of them shot at the line. Several soldiers from the line answered. The Chechens pulled back and the shooting stopped. But when Poltoratsky arrived with his company, he gave the order to fire, and as soon as the command was passed on, the merry, bracing crackle of muskets was heard all along the line, accompanied by prettily dispersing puffs of smoke. The soldiers, glad of a diversion, hurriedly reloaded and fired off round after round. The Chechens obviously took up the challenge and, leaping forward one after another, fired off several shots at the soldiers. One of their shots wounded a soldier. This soldier was that same Avdeev who had been at the listening post. When his comrades went over to him, he was lying facedown, holding the wound in his stomach with both hands and rocking rhythmically.

"I was just starting to load my musket, and I heard a thwack," the soldier paired with him was saying. "I looked: he let his musket drop."

Avdeev was from Poltoratsky's company. Seeing a bunch of soldiers gathered, Poltoratsky rode up to them.

"What, brother, been hit?" he said. "Where?"

Avdeev did not reply.

"I was just starting to load, Your Honor," the soldier paired with Avdeev began to say, "I heard a thwack, I looked—he let his musket drop."

"Tsk, tsk," Poltoratsky clucked his tongue. "Does it hurt, Avdeev?"

"It doesn't hurt, but it won't let me walk. I could use a drink, Your Honor."

They found some vodka, that is, the alcohol the soldiers used to drink in the Caucasus, and Panov, frowning sternly, offered it to Avdeev in the bottle cap. Avdeev began to drink, but pushed the cap away at once with his hand.

"My soul won't take it," he said. "You drink it."

Panov finished the alcohol. Avdeev again tried to get up and again sat down. They spread out a greatcoat and laid Avdeev on it.

"Your Honor, the colonel's coming," the sergeant major said to Poltoratsky.

"Well, all right, you see to it," said Poltoratsky and, brandishing his whip, he rode at a long trot to meet Vorontsov.

Vorontsov was riding his English thoroughbred bay stallion, accompanied by the regimental adjutant, a Cossack, and a Chechen interpreter.

"What's going on here?" he asked Poltoratsky.

"A party of them came and attacked the line," Poltoratsky answered him.

"Well, well, so you started it all."

"Not me, Prince," said Poltoratsky, smiling. "They were spoiling for it."

"I heard a soldier's been wounded?"

"Yes, very sad. A good soldier."

"Seriously?"

"Seems so—in the stomach."

"And do you know where I'm going?" asked Vorontsov.

"No, I don't."

"You really can't guess?"

"No."

"Hadji Murat has come over and is going to meet us right now."

"It can't be!"

"Yesterday an emissary came from him," said Vorontsov, barely suppressing a smile of joy. "He's supposed to be waiting for me right now at the Shalinskoe clearing. Post your riflemen as far as the clearing and then come to me."

"Yes, sir," said Poltoratsky, putting his hand to his papakha, and he rode to his company. He himself led the line along the right side and ordered the sergeant major to do the same on the left side. Meanwhile four soldiers carried the wounded man to the fortress.

Poltoratsky was already on his way back to Vorontsov when he saw some horsemen overtaking him from behind. Poltoratsky stopped and waited for them.

At the head of them all, on a white-maned horse, in a white cherkeska, in a papakha with a turban, and with gold-inlaid arms, rode a man of imposing appearance. This man was Hadji Murat. He rode up to Poltoratsky and said something to him in Tartar. Poltoratsky raised his eyebrows, spread his arms in a sign that he did not understand, and smiled. Hadji Murat answered his smile with a smile, and that smile struck

Poltoratsky by its childlike good nature. Poltoratsky had never expected this fearsome mountaineer to be like that. He had expected to see a gloomy, dry, alien man, and before him was a most simple man, who smiled such a kindly smile that he seemed not alien, but a long-familiar friend. Only one thing was peculiar about him: this was his wide-set eyes, which looked attentively, keenly, and calmly into the eyes of other people.

Hadji Murat's suite consisted of four men. In that suite was Khan Mahoma, the one who had gone to Vorontsov the night before. He was a red-cheeked, round-faced man with bright, black, lidless eyes, radiant with an expression of the joy of life. There was also a stocky, hairy man with joined eyebrows. This was the Tavlin Hanefi, who managed all of Hadji Murat's belongings. He was leading a spare horse with tightly packed saddlebags. Two men especially stood out among the suite: one young, slender as a woman in the waist and broad in the shoulders, with a barely sprouting blond beard, a handsome man with sheep's eyes—this was Eldar; and the other, blind in one eye, with no eyebrows or lashes, with a trimmed red beard and a scar across his nose and face—the Chechen Gamzalo.

Poltoratsky pointed out Vorontsov for Hadji Murat as he appeared down the road. Hadji Murat headed towards him and, coming close, put his right hand to his chest, said something in Tartar, and stopped. The Chechen interpreter translated:

" 'I surrender myself,' he says, 'to the will of the Russian tsar. I wish to serve him,' he says. 'I have long wished it,' he says. 'Shamil would not let me.' "

Having heard out the interpreter, Vorontsov offered his suede-gloved hand to Hadji Murat. Hadji Murat looked at this hand, paused for a second, but then pressed it firmly and said something more, looking now at the interpreter, now at Vorontsov.

"He says he did not want to come over to anyone but you, because you are the sardar's son. He respects you firmly."

Vorontsov nodded as a sign that he thanked him. Hadji Murat said something more, pointing to his suite.

"He says these people, his murids, will serve the Russians just as he will."

Vorontsov turned to look and nodded to them, too.

The merry, black-eyed, lidless Khan Mahoma, nodding in the same way, said something to Vorontsov that must have been funny, because the hairy Avar bared his bright white teeth in a smile. The red-haired Gamzalo only flashed his one red eye for an instant at Vorontsov and again fixed it on his horse's ears.

As Vorontsov and Hadji Murat, accompanied by the suite, rode back to the fortress, the soldiers taken from the line, gathering in a bunch, made their observations:

"He's been the ruin of so many souls, curse him, and now just think how they'll oblige him," said one.

"And what else? He was Shammel's top lootnant. Now, I bet . . ."

"He's a brave dzhigit, there's no denying."

"And the redhead, the redhead, now—looks sideways, like a beast."

"Ugh! Must be a real dog."

They all took special notice of the redhead.

WHERE THE WOODCUTTING WAS going on, the soldiers who were closer to the road ran out to have a look. An officer yelled at them, but Vorontsov told him to stop.

"Let them look at their old acquaintance. Do you know who this is?" Vorontsov asked a soldier standing closer by, articulating the words slowly with his English accent.

"No, Your Excellency."

"Hadji Murat—heard of him?"

"How could I not, Your Excellency, we beat him many times."

"Well, well, and you got it from him, too."

"That we did, Your Excellency," the soldier replied, pleased that he had managed to talk with his commander.

Hadji Murat understood that they were talking about him, and a merry smile lit up in his eyes. Vorontsov returned to the fortress in the most cheerful spirits.

VI

VORONTSOV WAS very pleased that he, precisely he, had managed to lure out and receive the chief, the most powerful enemy of Russia, after Shamil. There was only one unpleasant thing: the commander of the army in Vozdvizhenskoe was General Meller-Zakomelsky, and in fact the whole affair should have been conducted through him. But Vorontsov had done everything himself, without reporting to him, which might lead to unpleasantness. And this thought poisoned Vorontsov's pleasure a little.

On reaching his house, Vorontsov entrusted the murids to the regimental adjutant and led Hadji Murat into the house himself.

Princess Marya Vassilievna, dressed up, smiling, together with her son, a handsome, curly-headed, six-year-old boy, met Hadji Murat in the drawing room, and Hadji Murat, pressing his hands to his chest, said somewhat solemnly, through the interpreter who accompanied him, that he considered himself the prince's kunak, since the prince had received him into his house, and a kunak's whole family was as sacred for a kunak as he himself. Marya Vassilievna liked both the appearance and the manners of Hadji Murat. That he blushed when she gave him her big white hand disposed her still more in his favor. She invited him to sit down and, having asked him whether he drank coffee, ordered it served. However, Hadji Murat declined coffee when it was served to him. He had a little understanding of Russian, but could not speak it, and, when he did not understand, he smiled, and Marya Vassilievna liked his smile, just as Poltoratsky had. And Marya Vassilievna's curly-headed, sharp-eyed little son, whom she called Bulka, standing by his mother, did not take his eyes from Hadji Murat, whom he had heard of as an extraordinary warrior.

Leaving Hadji Murat with his wife, Vorontsov went to his office to make arrangements for informing his superiors about Hadji Murat's coming over. Having written a report to the commander of the left flank, General Kozlovsky, in Grozny, and a letter to his father, Vorontsov hurried home, fearing his wife's displeasure at having a strange, frightening man foisted on her, who had to be treated so that he was neither offended nor overly encouraged. But his fear was needless. Hadji Murat was sitting in an armchair holding Bulka, Vorontsov's stepson, on his knee, and, inclining his head, was listening attentively to what the interpreter was saying to him, conveying the words of the laughing Marya Vassilievna. Marya Vassilievna was telling him that if he were to give every kunak whatever thing of his the kunak praised, he would soon be going around like Adam . . .

When the prince came in, Hadji Murat took Bulka, who was surprised and offended by it, from his knee, and stood up, immediately changing the playful expression on his face to a stern and serious one. He sat down only when Vorontsov sat down. Continuing the conversation, he replied to Marya Vassilievna's words by saying that it was their law, that whatever a kunak likes must be given to the kunak.

"Your son—my kunak," he said in Russian, stroking the curly head of Bulka, who again climbed on his knee.

"He's charming, your brigand," Marya Vassilievna said to her husband in French. "Bulka admired his dagger, and he gave it to him."

Bulka showed his stepfather the dagger.

"C'est un objet de prix," said Marya Vassilievna.

*"Il faudra trouver l'occasion pour lui faire cadeau,"** said Vorontsov.

Hadji Murat sat with lowered eyes and, stroking the boy's curly head, repeated:

"Dzhigit, dzhigit."

"A beautiful dagger, beautiful," said Vorontsov, half drawing the sharp steel dagger with a groove down the middle. "Thank you."

"Ask him whether I can be of service to him," Vorontsov said to the interpreter.

The interpreter translated, and Hadji Murat replied at once that he did not need anything, but asked that he now be taken to a place where he could pray. Vorontsov called a valet and told him to carry out Hadji Murat's wish.

As soon as Hadji Murat was left alone in the room he was taken to, his face changed: the expression of pleasure and of alternating affection and solemnity vanished, and a preoccupied expression appeared.

The reception Vorontsov had given him was far better than he had expected. But the better that reception was, the less Hadji Murat trusted Vorontsov and his officers. He feared everything: that he would be seized, put in chains, and sent to Siberia, or simply killed; and therefore he was on his guard.

Eldar came, and he asked him where the murids were quartered, where the horses were, and whether their weapons had been taken from them.

Eldar reported that the horses were in the prince's stable, the men had

* "It's a valuable thing."
"We'll have to find the occasion to make him a gift."

been quartered in a shed, their weapons had remained with them, and the interpreter had treated them to food and tea.

Perplexed, Hadji Murat shook his head and, having undressed, stood in prayer. When he finished, he ordered his silver dagger brought to him and, dressed and girded, sat crosslegged on the divan, waiting for what would happen.

At four o'clock he was called to the prince's for dinner.

Hadji Murat ate nothing at dinner except pilaf, which he served himself from the same place on the dish from which Marya Vassilievna had taken for herself.

"He's afraid we may poison him," Marya Vassilievna said to her husband. "He took from where I did." And she at once addressed Hadji Murat through the interpreter, asking when he would now pray again. Hadji Murat held up five fingers and pointed to the sun.

"Soon, in other words."

Vorontsov took out his Breguet[6] and pressed the release. The watch struck four and one quarter. Hadji Murat was obviously surprised by this chiming, and he asked to hear it chime again and to look at the watch.

*"Voilà l'occasion. Donnez-lui la montre,"** Marya Vassilievna said to her husband.

Vorontsov at once offered Hadji Murat the watch. Hadji Murat put his hand to his chest and took the watch. He pressed the release several times, listened, and shook his head approvingly.

After dinner Meller-Zakomelsky's adjutant was announced to the prince.

The adjutant informed the prince that when the general learned of Hadji Murat's coming over, he was very displeased that it had not been reported to him, and he requested that Hadji Murat be brought to him immediately. Vorontsov said that the general's order would be carried out, and, informing Hadji Murat through the interpreter of the general's request, asked him to go with him to Meller.

Marya Vassilievna, learning why the adjutant had come, understood at once that there might be trouble between her husband and the general, and, despite all her husband's protests, made ready to go to the general with her husband and Hadji Murat.

* "Here's the occasion. Give him the watch."

"Vous feriez beaucoup mieux de rester; c'est mon affaire, mais pas la vôtre."

*"Vous ne pouvez pas m'empêcher d'aller voir madame la générale."**

"You could do it some other time."

"I want to do it now."

There was no help for it. Vorontsov agreed, and all three of them went.

When they came in, Meller, with glum courtesy, conducted Marya Vassilievna to his wife, and told the adjutant to take Hadji Murat to the reception room and not let him go anywhere until he was ordered to.

"If you please," he said to Vorontsov, opening the door of his study and allowing the prince to go in ahead of him.

On entering the study, he stopped before the prince and, without inviting him to sit down, said:

"I am the military commander here, and therefore all negotiations with the enemy must be conducted through me. Why did you not inform me of Hadji Murat's coming over?"

"An emissary came to see me and announced Hadji Murat's wish to give himself up to me," Vorontsov replied, turning pale with agitation, expecting a rude outburst from the wrathful general and at the same time becoming infected by his wrath.

"I ask you, why did you not report it to me?"

"I intended to, Baron, but . . ."

"I am not 'Baron' to you, I am 'Your Excellency.' "

And here the baron's long-restrained irritation suddenly burst out. He voiced all that for a long time had been seething in his soul.

"I have not served my sovereign for twenty-seven years in order to have men who began their service yesterday, availing themselves of their family connections, make arrangements under my very nose about things that do not concern them."

"Your Excellency! I beg you not to speak unfairly," Vorontsov interrupted him.

"I am speaking fairly and will not allow . . ." the general spoke even more irritably.

* "You would do much better to stay here; this is my affair, not yours."
"You can't stop me from going to see the general's wife."

Just then Marya Vassilievna came in, rustling her skirts, followed by a rather small, modest lady, Meller-Zakomelsky's wife.

"Well, enough, Baron. Simon didn't mean to cause any unpleasantness," Marya Vassilievna began.

"I was not speaking of that, Princess . . ."

"Well, you know, we'd better just drop it. You know: a bad spat is better than a good quarrel. Oh, what am I saying! . . ." She laughed.

And the irate general gave in to the bewitching smile of the beauty. A smile flashed under his mustache.

"I admit I was wrong," said Vorontsov, "but . . ."

"Well, I got a bit heated myself," said Meller, and he offered the prince his hand.

Peace was established, and it was decided to leave Hadji Murat with Meller temporarily and then send him to the commander of the left flank.

Hadji Murat was sitting in the next room, and though he did not understand what they were saying, he understood what he needed to understand: that the argument was about him, that his coming over from Shamil was a matter of great importance for the Russians, and that therefore, if only they did not exile or kill him, he could demand much from them. Besides that, he understood that Meller-Zakomelsky, though he was superior in rank, did not have the significance that Vorontsov, his subordinate, had, and that Vorontsov was important, while Meller-Zakomelsky was not; and therefore, when Meller-Zakomelsky summoned Hadji Murat and began to question him, Hadji Murat bore himself proudly and solemnly, saying that he had come from the mountains to serve the white tsar, and that he would give an accounting of everything only to his sardar, that is, commander in chief, Prince Vorontsov, in Tiflis.

VII

THE WOUNDED AVDEEV WAS CARRIED to the hospital, housed in a small building with a plank roof at the exit from the fortress, and put on one of the empty beds in the common ward. There were four patients in the ward: one thrashing in typhoid fever; another pale, with blue under his eyes, sick with the ague, waiting for a paroxysm and yawning constantly;

and another two wounded in a raid some three weeks earlier—one in the hand (he was walking about), the other in the shoulder (he was sitting on the bed). All of them, except for the one with typhoid, surrounded the new arrival and questioned those who brought him.

"Sometimes they shoot like spilling peas and nothing happens, but here they fired maybe five shots in all," one of the bearers was telling them.

"His time had come!"

"Oh," Avdeev grunted loudly, struggling against the pain, when they began to put him on the bed. Once he was laid out, he frowned and did not groan any more, but only kept moving his feet. He held his wound with his hands and stared straight ahead fixedly.

A doctor came and ordered the wounded man turned over to see whether the bullet had come out the other side.

"What's this?" the doctor asked, pointing to the crisscrossed white scars on his back and behind.

"That's an old thing, Your Honor," Avdeev said, groaning.

These were the traces of his punishment for the money he drank up.

Avdeev was turned back over, and the doctor picked in his stomach with the probe for a long time and found the bullet, but could remove it. Having bandaged the wound and pasted a sticking plaster over it, the doctor left. All through the picking in the wound and the bandaging of it, Avdeev lay with clenched teeth and closed eyes. When the doctor left, he opened his eyes and looked around him in surprise. His eyes were directed at the patients and the orderly, but it was as if he did not see them, but saw something else that surprised him very much.

Avdeev's comrades came—Panov and Seryogin. Avdeev went on lying in the same way, gazing straight ahead in surprise. For a long time he could not recognize his comrades, though his eyes were looking straight at them.

"Don't you want to have somebody write home, Pyotr?" said Panov.

Avdeev did not answer, though he was looking at Panov's face.

"I said, don't you want to have somebody write home?" Panov asked again, touching his cold, broad-boned hand.

It was as if Avdeev came to.

"Ah, Antonych has come!"

"Yes, here I am. Don't you want to have somebody write home? Seryogin will write for you."

"Seryogin," said Avdeev, shifting his gaze with difficulty to Seryogin, "will you write? . . . Write this, then: 'Your son, Petrukha, wishes you long life.' I envied my brother. I told you today. But now I'm glad. I mean, let him live on and on. God grant it, I'm glad. Write that."

Having said that, he fell silent for a long time, his eyes fixed on Panov.

"Well, and did you find your pipe?" he suddenly asked.

Panov shook his head and did not answer.

"Your pipe, your pipe, I'm saying, did you find it?" Avdeev repeated.

"It was in my bag."

"So there. Well, and now give me a candle, I'll be dying," said Avdeev.

Just then Poltoratsky came to visit his soldier.

"What, brother, is it bad?" he said.

Avdeev closed his eyes and shook his head negatively. His high-cheekboned face was pale and stern. He said nothing in reply and only repeated again, addressing Panov:

"Give me a candle. I'll be dying."

They put a candle in his hand, but his fingers would not bend, so they stuck it between his fingers and held it there. Poltoratsky left, and five minutes after he left, the orderly put his ear to Avdeev's heart and said it was all over.

In the report sent to Tiflis, Avdeev's death was described in the following way: "On November 23rd two companies of the Kurinsky regiment went out of the fortress to cut wood. In the middle of the day, a considerable body of mountaineers suddenly attacked the woodcutters. The picket line began to drop back, and at that moment the second company fell upon the mountaineers with bayonets and overcame them. Two privates were lightly wounded in the action and one was killed. The mountaineers lost around a hundred men killed and wounded."

VIII

On the same day that Petrukha Avdeev was dying in the Vozdvizhenskoe hospital, his old father, the wife of his brother, for whom he had gone as a soldier, and the older brother's daughter, a girl of marriageable age, were threshing oats on the frozen threshing floor. Deep snow had fallen the day before, and towards morning it had become freezing cold.

The old man woke up at the third cockcrow and, seeing bright moonlight in the frosted window, got down from the stove,[7] put on his boots, his winter coat, his hat, and went to the threshing floor. After working there for some two hours, the old man went back to the cottage and woke up his son and the women. When the women and the girl came to the threshing floor, it had been cleared, a wooden shovel was stuck into the dry white snow and next to it a besom, twigs up, and the oat sheaves were laid out in two rows, ears to ears, in a long line across the clean floor. They sorted out the flails and began to beat in a measured rhythm of three strokes. The old man beat hard with his heavy flail, breaking up the straw, the girl beat steadily from above, the daughter-in-law knocked it aside.

The moon set, and it began to grow light; and they were already finishing the line when the elder son, Akim, in a short coat and hat, came out to the workers.

"What are you loafing about for?" the father shouted at him, interrupting the threshing and leaning on his flail.

"Somebody's got to tend to the horses."

"Tend to the horses," the father mimicked him. "The old woman'll tend to them. Take a flail. You've grown too fat. Drunkard!"

"Wasn't your drink, was it?" the son grumbled.

"What's that?" the old man asked menacingly, frowning and skipping a stroke.

The son silently took a flail, and the work went on with four flails: trap, tra-ta-tap, trap, tra-ta-tap . . . trap! The old man's heavy flail struck every fourth time.

"Just look at the nape on him, like some real, good squire. And I can't keep my pants up," the old man said, skipping a stroke and swinging the flail in the air so as not to lose the rhythm.

The line was finished, and the women started removing the straw with rakes.

"Petrukha's a fool to have gone for you. They'd have beaten the nonsense out of you in the army, and at home he was worth five the likes of you."

"Well, enough, father," the daughter-in-law said, throwing aside the broken sheaf binders.

"Yes, feed the five of you and there's not even one man's work from you. Petrukha used to work like two men by himself, not like . . ."

Down the beaten path from the yard, creaking over the snow in new bast shoes with tightly wrapped woolen footcloths under them, came the old woman. The men were raking the unwinnowed grain into a pile, the women and the girl were sweeping up.

"The headman came by. Everybody's got to go and transport bricks for the master," said the old woman. "I've made breakfast. Come along now."

"All right. Hitch up the roan and go," the old man said to Akim. "And see that I don't have to answer for you like the other day. Mind you of Petrukha."

"When he was at home, you yelled at him," Akim now snarled at his father, "but he's not, so you nag me."

"Means you deserve it," his mother said just as crossly. "You can't take Petrukha's place."

"Well, all right!" said the son.

"Oh, yes, all right. You drank up the flour, and now you say 'all right.' "

"Don't open old wounds," said the daughter-in-law, and they all laid down their flails and went to the house.

The friction between the father and the son had begun long ago, almost from the time when Pyotr was sent as a soldier. Even then the old man already sensed that he had exchanged a hawk for a cuckoo bird. True, according to the law, as the old man understood it, the childless son had to go in place of the family man. Akim had four children, Pyotr had none, but Pyotr was the same kind of worker as his father: skillful, keen-witted, strong, enduring, and, above all, industrious. He was always working. When he passed by people at work, just as his father used to do, he at once offered to help—to go a row or two with the scythe, or to load a cart, or to fell a tree, or to chop wood. The old man was sorry about him, but there was nothing to be done. Soldiering was like death. A soldier was a cut-off limb, and to remember him—to chafe your soul—was useless. Only rarely did the old man remember him, like today, in order to needle the elder son. But the mother often remembered her younger son, and for two years now she had been asking the old man to send Petrukha some money. But the old man kept silent.

The Avdeevs' farmstead was rich, and the old man had a bit of cash tucked away, but he would not venture to touch what he had saved for anything. Now, when the old woman heard him mention the younger son, she decided to ask him again to send their son at least one little rouble once the oats were sold. And so she did. Left alone with the old man once the younger people went to work for the master, she persuaded him to send one rouble of the oat money to Petrukha. So that, when the piles had been winnowed and twelve quarters of oats had been poured on sheets of burlap in three sledges, and the sheets had been neatly pinned with wooden pins, she gave her old man a letter written in her words by the village clerk, and the old man promised that in town he would put a rouble into the letter and send it.

The old man, dressed in a new fur coat and a kaftan, and in clean white woolen leggings, took the letter, put it in his pouch, and, having prayed to God, got into the front sledge and went to town. His grandson rode in the rear sledge. In town the old man told the innkeeper to read him the letter and listened to it attentively and approvingly.

In her letter Petrukha's mother sent, first, her blessing, second, greetings from them all, the news of his godfather's death, and at the end the news that Aksinya (Pyotr's wife) "did not want to live with us and went off on her own. We hear that she lives a good and honorable life." There was mention of the present, the rouble, and added to that, word for word, was what the rueful old woman, with tears in her eyes, had told the clerk to write straight from her heart:

"And so, dear little child of mine, my little dove Petrushenka, I've wept my eyes out grieving over you. My beloved little sun, why did you leave me . . ." At this point the old woman had begun to wail and weep, and said:

"Leave it like that."

It remained like that in the letter, but Petrukha was not fated to receive either the news that his wife had left home, or the rouble, or his mother's last words. The letter and the money came back with the news that Petrukha had been killed in the war, "defending the tsar, the fatherland, and the Orthodox faith." So wrote the army scribe.

The old woman, on receiving this news, wailed for as long as she had time, and then got back to work. On the first Sunday she went to church and handed out little pieces of communion bread "to the good people in memory of the servant of God Pyotr."

The soldier's wife Aksinya also wailed on learning of the death of her "beloved husband" with whom she had "lived only one little year." She pitied both her husband and all her own ruined life. And in her wailing she mentioned "Pyotr Mikhailovich's light brown curls, and his love, and her wretched life with the orphan Vanka," and bitterly reproached "Petrusha for pitying his brother and not pitying wretched her, a wanderer among strangers."

But deep in her heart Aksinya was glad of Pyotr's death. She was pregnant again by the salesclerk she lived with, and now no one could reproach her anymore, and the salesclerk could marry her, as he had said he would when he was persuading her to love him.

IX

MIKHAIL SEMYONOVICH VORONTSOV,[8] brought up in England, the son of the Russian ambassador, was a man of European education rare at that time among highly placed Russian officials, ambitious, mild and gentle in his dealings with his inferiors, and a subtle courtier in his relations with his superiors. He could not understand life without power and obedience. He had all the highest ranks and decorations and was considered a skillful military man, even as the vanquisher of Napoleon at Craonne.[9] In the year 1851 he was over seventy, but he was still quite fresh, moved briskly, and above all was in full possession of all the adroitness of a fine and pleasant intelligence, directed at the maintaining of his power and the strengthening and spreading of his popularity. He possessed great wealth—both his own and that of his wife, Countess Branitsky—and received an enormous maintenance in his quality as vicegerent, and spent the greater part of his means on the construction of a palace and garden on the southern coast of the Crimea.

On the evening of 7 December 1851, a courier's troika drove up to his palace in Tiflis. A weary officer, all black with dust, bringing news from General Kozlovsky that Hadji Murat had come over to the Russians, stretching his legs, walked past the sentries onto the wide porch of the vicegerent's palace. It was six o'clock in the evening, and Vorontsov was about to go to dinner when the courier's arrival was announced to him. Vorontsov received the courier without delay and was therefore several minutes late for dinner. When he entered the dining room, the dinner guests, some thirty of them, sitting around Princess Elizaveta Ksaverievna or standing in groups by the windows, rose and turned their faces towards him. Vorontsov was in his usual black military tunic without epaulettes, with narrow shoulder straps and a white cross on his neck. His clean-shaven, foxy face smiled pleasantly, and his eyes narrowed as he looked over the whole gathering.

Having entered the dining room with soft, hurrying steps, he apologized to the ladies for being late, greeted the men, and went up to the Georgian princess Manana Orbeliani, a full-bodied, tall, forty-five-year-old beauty of the Oriental type, and gave her his arm to lead her to the table. Princess Elizaveta Ksaverievna herself took the arm of a visiting reddish-haired general with bristling mustaches. The Georgian prince gave his arm to Countess Choiseul, the princess's friend. Doctor Andreevsky, the adjutants, and others, some with, some without ladies, followed the three couples. Footmen in kaftans, stockings, and shoes pulled out and pushed back the chairs, seating them; the head waiter solemnly ladled steaming soup from a silver tureen.

Vorontsov sat at the middle of the long table. Across from him sat his wife, with the general. To his right was his lady, the beautiful Orbeliani; to his left, a slender, dark-haired, red-cheeked young Georgian princess in glittering jewelry, who never stopped smiling.

"Excellentes, chère amie," Vorontsov replied to the princess's question of what news he had received from the courier. *"Simon a eu de la chance."**

And he began to tell, so that all those sitting at the table could hear, the astounding news—for him alone it was not entirely news, because the negotiations had long been going on—that the famous Hadji Murat, the bravest of Shamil's lieutenants, had come over to the Russians and would be brought to Tiflis today or tomorrow.

All the dinner guests, even the young men, adjutants and clerks, who sat at the far ends of the table and had been quietly laughing about something just before, became silent and listened.

"And you, General, have you met this Hadji Murat?" the princess asked her neighbor, the red-haired general with bristling mustaches, when the prince finished speaking.

"More than once, Princess."

* Excellent, my dear friend... Simon has been lucky.

And the general told how, in the year forty-three, after the mountaineers had taken Gergebil, Hadji Murat had happened upon General Passek's detachment, and how he had killed Colonel Zolotukhin almost before their eyes.

Vorontsov listened to the general with an agreeable smile, obviously pleased that the general was talking. But suddenly Vorontsov's face assumed a distracted and glum expression.

The talkative general began to tell about where he had met Hadji Murat the second time.

"It was he," the general was saying, "kindly remember, Your Excellency, who set up an ambush on the rescue during the biscuit expedition."

"Where?" Vorontsov asked, narrowing his eyes.

The thing was that what the brave general referred to as the "rescue" was that action during the unfortunate Dargo campaign, in which an entire detachment, with its commander, Prince Vorontsov, would indeed have perished, if fresh troops had not come to their rescue. It was known to everyone that the entire Dargo campaign, under Vorontsov's command, in which the Russians suffered great losses in killed and wounded and several cannon, was a shameful event, and therefore if anyone did talk about that campaign in front of Vorontsov, it was only in the sense in which Vorontsov had written his report to the tsar, that is, that it had been a brilliant exploit of the Russian army. But the word "rescue" pointed directly to the fact that it had been, not a brilliant exploit, but a mistake that had destroyed many men. Everyone understood that, and some pretended that they had not caught the meaning of the general's words, others waited fearfully for what would happen next; a few smiled and exchanged glances.

Only the red-haired general with the bristling mustaches noticed nothing and, carried away by his story, calmly replied:

"On the rescue, Your Excellency."

And once launched upon his favorite theme, the general told in detail how "this Hadji Murat had so deftly cut the detachment in two that, if it hadn't been for the 'rescue' "—he seemed to repeat the word "rescue" with a special fondness—"we'd all have stayed there, because . . ."

The general did not manage to finish, because Manana Orbeliani, realizing what was the matter, interrupted the general's speech, asking him about the comforts of his accomodations in Tiflis. The general was surprised, looked around at them all and at his adjutant at the end of the table, who was looking at him with a fixed and meaningful gaze—and suddenly understood. Without answering the princess, he frowned, fell silent, and hurriedly started eating, without chewing, the delicacy that lay on his plate, incomprehensible in look and even in taste.

Everyone felt awkward, but the awkwardness of the situation was remedied by the Georgian prince, very stupid, but a remarkably subtle and skillful flatterer and courtier, who was sitting on the other side of Princess Vorontsov. As if he had not noticed anything, he began telling in a loud voice about Hadji Murat's abduction of the widow of Akhmet Khan of Mekhtulin.

"He came into the village at night, seized what he wanted, and rode off with his entire party."

"Why did he want precisely that woman?" asked the princess.

"He was her husband's enemy, pursued him, but was never able to confront the khan before his death, so he took revenge on the widow."

The princess translated this into French for her old friend, Countess Choiseul, who was sitting next to the Georgian prince.

*"Quelle horreur!"** said the countess, closing her eyes and shaking her head.

"Oh, no," Vorontsov said, smiling, "I was told that he treated his prisoner with chivalrous respect and then released her."

"Yes, for a ransom."

"Well, of course, but even so he acted nobly."

The prince's words set the tone for the further stories told about Hadji Murat. The courtiers understood that the more importance they ascribed to Hadji Murat, the more pleased Prince Vorontsov would be.

"Amazing boldness the man has. A remarkable man."

"Why, in the year forty-nine he burst into Temir Khan Shura in broad daylight and looted the shops."

An Armenian man sitting at the end of the table, who had been in Temir Khan Shura at the time, told in detail about this exploit of Hadji Murat's.

Generally, the whole dinner passed in telling stories about Hadji Murat. They all vied with each other in praising his courage, intelli-

* How horrible!

gence, magnanimity. Someone told how he had ordered twenty-six prisoners killed; but to this there was the usual objection:

"No help for it! *À la guerre comme à la guerre.*"*

"He's a great man."

"If he'd been born in Europe, he might have been a new Napoleon," said the stupid Georgian prince with the gift for flattery.

He knew that every mention of Napoleon, for the victory over whom Vorontsov wore a white cross on his neck, was pleasing to the prince.

"Well, maybe not Napoleon, but a dashing cavalry general—yes," said Vorontsov.

"If not Napoleon, then Murat."[10]

"And his name is Hadji Murat."

"Hadji Murat has come over, now it's the end of Shamil," someone said.

"They feel that now" (this "now" meant under Vorontsov) "they won't hold out," said someone else.

"*Tout cela est grâce à vous,*"† said Manana Orbeliani.

Prince Vorontsov tried to keep down the waves of flattery that were already beginning to inundate him. But it was pleasant for him, and he escorted his lady to the drawing room in the best of spirits.

After dinner, when coffee was served in the drawing room, the prince was especially amiable with everyone and, going up to the general with red, bristling mustaches, tried to show him that he had not noticed his awkwardness.

Having made the round of all his guests, the prince sat down to cards. He played only the old-fashioned game of ombre. The prince's partners were the Georgian prince, then the Armenian general, who had learned to play ombre from the prince's valet, and the fourth—famous for his power—Dr. Andreevsky.

Placing a gold snuffbox with a portrait of Alexander I beside him, Vorontsov cracked the deck of satiny cards and was about to deal them when his valet, the Italian Giovanni, came in with a letter on a silver salver.

"Another courier, Your Excellency."

* War is war.

† All that is thanks to you.

Vorontsov put down the cards and, apologizing, unsealed the letter and began to read.

The letter was from his son. He described Hadji Murat's coming over and his own confrontation with Meller-Zakomelsky.

The princess came over and asked what their son wrote.

"The same thing. *Il a eu quelques désagréments avec le commandant de la place. Simon a eu tort.** But all is well that ends well," he said in English, and, turning to his respectfully waiting partners, he asked them to take their cards.

When the first hand had been dealt, Vorontsov opened the snuffbox and did what he always did when he was in especially good spirits: he took a pinch of French tobacco with his old man's wrinkled white hand, put it to his nose, and snuffed it in.

X

WHEN HADJI MURAT PRESENTED himself to Vorontsov the next day, the prince's anteroom was full of people. There was yesterday's general with the bristling mustaches, in full-dress uniform and decorations, come to take his leave; there was a regimental commander who was threatened with court action for abuses to do with regimental provisions; there was a rich Armenian, patronized by Dr. Andreevsky, who held the monopoly on vodka and was now soliciting for the renewal of his contract; there, all in black, was the widow of an officer who had been killed, come to ask for a pension or for child support from the state treasury; there was a ruined Georgian prince in magnificent Georgian dress, soliciting for some abandoned Church property; there was a district police commissioner with a big packet containing plans for a new way of subjugating the Caucasus; there was a khan who came only so as to be able to tell them at home that he had called upon the prince.

They all waited their turn and one after another were shown into the prince's office by a handsome, fair-haired young adjutant.

When Hadji Murat, at a brisk stride, limping slightly, came into the

* He had some unpleasantness with the local commandant. Simon was in the wrong.

anteroom, all eyes turned to him, and from various sides he heard his name spoken in a whisper.

Hadji Murat was dressed in a long white cherkeska over a brown beshmet with fine silver piping on its collar. On his legs there were black leggings and on his feet matching chuviaki that fitted them like a glove, on his shaven head a papakha with a turban—the same for which, on the denunciation of Akhmet Khan, he had been arrested by General Klugenau,[11] and which had been the reason for his going over to Shamil. Hadji Murat walked in, stepping briskly over the parquet of the anteroom, his whole slender body swaying from the slight lameness of one leg, which was shorter than the other. His wide-set eyes looked calmly before him and seemed not to notice anyone.

The handsome adjutant, having greeted him, asked Hadji Murat to sit down while he announced him to the prince. But Hadji Murat declined to sit down and, putting his hand behind his dagger and advancing one foot, went on standing, scornfully looking around at those present.

The interpreter, Prince Tarkhanov, came up to Hadji Murat and began speaking to him. Hadji Murat replied reluctantly, curtly. A Kumyk prince, who had a complaint against a police commissioner, came out of the office, and after him the adjutant called Hadji Murat, led him to the door of the office, and showed him in.

Vorontsov received Hadji Murat standing by the edge of his desk. The old white face of the commander in chief was not smiling, as the day before, but rather stern and solemn.

On entering the big room, with its enormous desk and big windows with green jalousies, Hadji Murat put his small, sunburnt hands to the place on his chest where the edges of his white cherkeska overlapped and, unhurriedly, clearly, and respectfully, in the Kumyk dialect, which he spoke well, lowering his eyes, said:

"I place myself under the great tsar's high protection and your own. I promise to serve the white tsar faithfully, to the last drop of my blood, and I hope to be of use in the war with Shamil, my enemy and yours."

Having listened to the interpreter, Vorontsov glanced at Hadji Murat, and Hadji Murat glanced into Vorontsov's face.

The eyes of these two men, as they met, said much to each other that could not be expressed in words and that certainly was not what the interpreter was saying. They spoke the whole truth about each other directly, without words. Vorontsov's eyes said that he did not believe a single word of all that Hadji Murat had said, that he knew he was the enemy of all things Russian, would always remain so, and was submitting now only because he had been forced to do so. And Hadji Murat understood that and all the same assured him of his fidelity. Hadji Murat's eyes said that this old man ought to be thinking about death, and not about war, but though he was old, he was cunning, and one had to be careful with him. And Vorontsov understood that and all the same said to Hadji Murat what he considered necessary for the success of the war.

"Tell him," Vorontsov said to the interpreter (he spoke informally to the young officer), "that our sovereign is as merciful as he is mighty, and probably, at my request, will pardon him and take him into his service. Did you tell him?" he asked, looking at Hadji Murat. "Tell him that, until I receive the merciful decision of my ruler, I take it upon myself to receive him and make his stay with us agreeable."

Hadji Murat once more put his hands to the middle of his chest and began to say something animatedly.

He said, as conveyed by the interpreter, that formerly, when he ruled Avaria, in the year thirty-nine, he served the Russians faithfully and would never have betrayed them if it had not been for his enemy Akhmet Khan, who wanted to ruin him and slandered him before General Klugenau.

"I know, I know," said Vorontsov (though if he had known, he had long forgotten it all). "I know," he said, sitting down and pointing Hadji Murat to the divan that stood by the wall. But Hadji Murat did not sit down, shrugging his strong shoulders as a sign that he would not venture to sit in the presence of such an important man.

"Akhmet Khan and Shamil are both my enemies," he went on, turning to the interpreter. "Tell the prince: Akhmet Khan died, I could not be revenged on him, but Shamil is still alive, and I will not die before I have repaid him," he said, frowning and tightly clenching his jaws.

"Yes, yes," Vorontsov said calmly. "But how does he want to repay Shamil?" he said to the interpreter. "And tell him that he may sit down."

Hadji Murat again declined to sit down and, to the question conveyed to him, replied that he had come over to the Russians in order to help them to destroy Shamil.

"Fine, fine," said Vorontsov. "But precisely what does he want to do? Sit down, sit down . . ."

Hadji Murat sat down and said that, if they would only send him to the Lezghian line and give him an army, he guaranteed that he would raise the whole of Daghestan, and Shamil would be unable to hold out.

"That's fine. That's possible," said Vorontsov. "I'll think about it."

The interpreter conveyed Vorontsov's words to Hadji Murat. Hadji Murat fell to thinking.

"Tell the sardar," he said further, "that my family is in my enemy's hands; and as long as my family is in the mountains, my hands are tied and I cannot serve him. He will kill my wife, kill my mother, kill my children, if I go against him directly. Let the prince only rescue my family, exchange them for prisoners, and then I will either die or destroy Shamil."

"Fine, fine," said Vorontsov. "We'll think about that. And now let him go to the chief of staff and explain to him in detail his situation, his intentions and wishes."

So ended Hadji Murat's first meeting with Vorontsov.

In the evening of that same day, in the new theater decorated in Oriental taste, an Italian opera was playing. Vorontsov was in his box, and in the parterre appeared the conspicuous figure of the lame Hadji Murat in his turban. He came in with Vorontsov's adjutant, Loris-Melikov,[12] who had been attached to him, and took a seat in the front row. With Oriental, Muslim dignity, not only with no expression of surprise, but with an air of indifference, having sat through the first act, Hadji Murat stood up and, calmly looking around at the spectators, went out, drawing the attention of all the spectators to himself.

The next day was Monday, the habitual soirée at the Vorontsovs'. In the big, brightly lit hall an orchestra, hidden in the winter garden, was playing. Young and not-so-young women, in dresses baring their necks, their arms, and almost their breasts, turned in the arms of men in bright uniforms. By the mountains of snacks, valets in red tailcoats, stockings, and shoes, poured champagne and went about offering sweets to the ladies. The wife of the "sardar," also just as half-bared, despite her no longer young years, walked among the guests, smiling affably, and, through the interpreter, said a few amiable words to Hadji Murat, who, with the same indifference as the day before in the theater, was looking the guests over. After the hostess, other bared women came up to Hadji Murat, and all of them, unashamed, stood before him and, smiling, asked one and the same thing: how did he like what he saw. Vorontsov himself, in gold epaulettes and aglets, with the white cross on his neck and a ribbon, came up to him and asked the same thing, obviously convinced, like all the questioners, that Hadji Murat could not help liking all he saw. And Hadji Murat gave Vorontsov the same answer he gave them all: that his people did not have it—without saying whether it was good or bad that they did not have it.

Hadji Murat tried to talk with Vorontsov even here, at the ball, about the matter of ransoming his family, but Vorontsov, pretending that he had not heard his words, walked away from him. Loris-Melikov said later to Hadji Murat that this was not the place to talk business.

When it struck eleven and Hadji Murat verified the time on his watch, given to him by Marya Vassilievna, he asked Loris-Melikov whether he could leave. Loris-Melikov said he could, but it would be better to stay. In spite of that, Hadji Murat did not stay and drove off in the phaeton put at his disposal to the quarters assigned to him.

XI

On the fifth day of Hadji Murat's stay in Tiflis, Loris-Melikov, the vicegerent's adjutant, came to him on orders from the commander in chief.

"My head and my hands are glad to serve the sardar," said Hadji Murat with his usual diplomatic expression, bowing his head and putting his hands to his chest. "Order me," he said, glancing amiably into Loris-Melikov's eyes.

Loris-Melikov sat in an armchair that stood by the table. Hadji Murat seated himself on a low divan facing him and, his hands propped on his knees, bowed his head and began listening attentively to what Loris-Melikov said to him. Loris-Melikov, who spoke Tartar fluently, said that the prince, though he knew Hadji Murat's past, wished to learn his whole story from him.

"You tell it to me," said Loris-Melikov, "and I will write it down, then translate it into Russian, and the prince will send it to the sovereign."

Hadji Murat paused (he not only never interrupted anyone's speech, but always waited to see if his interlocutor was going to say something more), then raised his head, shook back his papakha, and smiled that special childlike smile that had already captivated Marya Vassilievna.

"That is possible," he said, obviously flattered by the thought that his story would be read by the sovereign.

"Tell it to me," Loris-Melikov said to him informally (in Tartar there is no formal address), "right from the beginning, and don't hurry." And he took a notebook from his pocket.

"That is possible, only there is much, very much to tell. Many things happened," said Hadji Murat.

"If you don't manage in one day, you can finish the next," said Loris-Melikov.

"Begin from the beginning?"

"Yes, from the very beginning: where you were born, where you lived."

Hadji Murat lowered his head and sat like that for a long time; then he picked up a little stick that lay by the divan, took from under his dagger with its gold-mounted ivory hilt a razor-sharp steel knife and began to whittle the stick with it and at the same time to tell his story:

"Write: Born in Tselmes, a small aoul, the size of an ass's head, as we say in the mountains," he began. "Not far from us, a couple of shots away, was Khunzakh, where the khans lived. And our family was close to them. My mother nursed the eldest khan, Abununtsal Khan, which is why I became close to the khans. There were three khans: Abununtsal Khan, the foster brother of my brother Osman, Umma Khan, my sworn brother, and Bulatch Khan, the youngest, the one Shamil threw from the cliff. But of that later. I was about fifteen years old when the murids started going around the aouls. They struck the stones with wooden sabers and cried: 'Muslims, ghazavat!' All the Chechens went over to the murids, and the Avars began to go over. I lived in the palace then. I was like a brother to the khans: I did as I liked and became rich. I had horses, and weapons, and I had money. I lived for my own pleasure, not thinking about anything. And I lived like that till the time when Kazi Mullah was killed and Hamzat stood in his place.[13] Hamzat sent envoys to the khans to tell them that, if they did not take up the ghazavat, he would lay waste to Khunzakh. This needed thought. The khans were afraid of the Russians, afraid to take up the ghazavat, and the khansha sent me with her son, the second one, Umma Khan, to Tiflis, to ask the chief Russian commander for help against Hamzat. The chief commander was Rosen, the baron. He did not receive me or Umma Khan. He sent to tell us he would help and did nothing. Only his officers began coming to us and playing cards with Umma Khan. They got him drunk and took him to bad places, and he lost all he had to them at cards. He was strong as a bull in body, and brave as a lion, but his soul was weak as water. He would have gambled away his last horses and weapons, if I hadn't taken him away. After Tiflis my thinking changed, and I began to persuade the khansha and the young khans to take up the ghazavat."

"Why did your thinking change?" asked Loris-Melikov. "You didn't like the Russians?"

Hadji Murat paused.

"No, I didn't," he said resolutely and closed his eyes. "And there was something else that made me want to take up the ghazavat."

"What was that?"

"Near Tselmes the khan and I ran into three murids: two got away, but the third I killed with my pistol. When I went up to him to take his weapons, he was still alive. He looked at me. 'You have killed me,' he said. 'That is well with me. But you are a Muslim, and young and strong. Take up the ghazavat. God orders it.' "

"Well, and did you take it up?"

"I didn't, but I started thinking," said Hadji Murat, and he went on with his story. "When Hamzat approached Khunzakh, we sent some old men and told them to say that we were ready to take up the ghazavat, if only he would send a learned man to explain how we were to keep it. Hamzat ordered the old men's mustaches shaved, their nostrils pierced, and flat cakes hung from their noses, and sent them back. The old men said that Hamzat was ready to send a sheikh to teach us the ghazavat, but only if the khansha sent her youngest son to him as an amanat. The khansha trusted Hamzat and sent Bulatch Khan to him. Hamzat received Bulatch Khan well, and sent to us to invite the older brothers, too. He told the messenger to say that he wanted to serve the khans just as his father had served their father. The khansha was a weak woman, foolish and bold, as all women are when they live by their own will. She was afraid to send both her sons, and sent only Umma Khan. I went with him. The murids rode out a mile ahead to meet us, and sang, and fired their guns, and caracoled around us. And when we rode up, Hamzat came out of his tent, went to the stirrup of Umma Khan, and received him as befits a khan. He said: 'I have done no harm to your house and do not want to. Only do not kill me and do not hinder me from bringing people over to the ghazavat. And I will serve you with my whole army as my father served your father. Let me live in your house. I will help you with my advice, and you do what you want.' Umma Khan was dull of speech. He did not know what to say, and was silent. Then I said, if it was so, let Hamzat go to Khunzakh. The khansha and the khan would receive him with honor. But they did not let me finish, and here for the first time I encountered Shamil. He was right there by the imam. 'It was not you who were asked, but the khan,' he said to me. I fell silent, and Hamzat took Umma Khan to the tent. Then Hamzat called me and told me to go to Khunzakh with his envoys. I went. The envoys started persuading the khansha to let the oldest khan go to Hamzat as well. I saw the treachery and told the khansha not to send her son. But a woman has as much sense in her head as there are hairs on an egg. She trusted them and told her son to go. Abununtsal did not want to. Then she said, 'It's clear you're afraid.' Like a bee, she knew where to sting him most painfully. Abununtsal flared up, did not speak any more with her, and ordered his horse saddled. I went with him. Hamzat met us still better than Umma Khan. He himself rode out two shots' distance down the hill. After him rode horsemen with standards, singing *'La ilaha il Allah,'* shooting off their guns, and caracoling. When we came to the camp, Hamzat led the khan into the tent. And I stayed with the horses. I was at the foot of the hill when shooting began in Hamzat's tent. I ran to the tent. Umma Khan lay face down in a pool of blood, and Abununtsal was fighting with the murids. Half his face had been cut off and hung down. He held it with one hand and held a dagger in the other, with which he cut down everyone who came near him. In front of me he cut down Hamzat's brother and turned against another man, but here the murids started shooting at him and he fell."

Hadji Murat stopped, his tanned face turned reddish brown, and his eyes became bloodshot.

"Fear came over me, and I ran away."

"Really?" said Loris-Melikov. "I thought you were never afraid of anything."

"Never afterwards. Since then I always remembered that shame, and when I remembered it, I was no longer afraid of anything."

XII

"ENOUGH FOR NOW. I must pray," said Hadji Murat, and he took Vorontsov's Breguet from the inside breast pocket of his cherkeska, carefully pressed the release, and, inclining his head to one side and repressing a childlike smile, listened. The watch rang twelve and a quarter.

"Kunak Vorontsov peshkesh," he said, smiling. "A good man."

"Yes, a good man," said Loris-Melikov. "And a good watch. You go and pray, then, and I'll wait."

"*Yakshi*, good," said Hadji Murat, and he went to the bedroom.

Left alone, Loris-Melikov wrote down in his notebook the main things from what Hadji Murat had told him, then lit a cigarette and began pacing up and down the room. Coming to the door opposite the bedroom, Loris-Melikov heard the animated voices of people speaking about something rapidly in Tartar. He realized that these were Hadji Murat's murids and, opening the door, went in.

In the room there was that special sour, leathery smell that mountaineers usually have. On the floor, on a burka by the window, sat one-eyed, red-haired Gamzalo, in a ragged, greasy beshmet, plaiting a bridle. He was saying something heatedly in his hoarse voice, but when Loris-Melikov came in, he fell silent at once and, paying no attention to him, went on with what he was doing. Facing him stood the merry Khan Mahoma, baring his white teeth and flashing his black, lashless eyes, and repeating one and the same thing. The handsome Eldar, the sleeves rolled up on his strong arms, was rubbing the girth of a saddle that hung from a nail. Hanefi, the chief worker and household manager, was not in the room. He was in the kitchen cooking dinner.

"What were you arguing about?" Loris-Melikov asked Khan Mahoma, having greeted him.

"He keeps praising Shamil," said Khan Mahoma, giving Loris his hand. "He says Shamil is a great man. A scholar, and a holy man, and a dzhigit."

"But how is it that he left him and keeps praising him?"

"He left him, and he praises him," said Khan Mahoma, baring his teeth and flashing his eyes.

"And do you, too, regard him as a holy man?" asked Loris-Melikov.

"If he weren't a holy man, people wouldn't listen to him," said Gamzalo.

"The holy man was not Shamil, but Mansur,"[14] said Khan Mahoma. "That was a real holy man. When he was imam, all the people were different. He went around the aouls, and the people came out to him, kissed the skirts of his cherkeska, and repented of their sins, and swore not to do bad things. The old men said: Back then all the people lived like holy men—didn't smoke, didn't drink, didn't miss prayers, forgave each other's offenses, even blood offenses. Back then, if they found money or things, they tied them to poles and set them up on the roads. Back then God granted the people success in all things, and it wasn't like now," said Khan Mahoma.

"Now, too, they don't drink or smoke in the mountains," said Gamzalo.

"Your Shamil is a lamoroi," said Khan Mahoma, winking at Loris-Melikov.

"Lamoroi" was a contemptuous name for the mountaineers.

"A lamoroi is a mountaineer. It's in the mountains that eagles live," replied Gamzalo.

"Good boy! A neat cut," said Khan Mahoma, baring his teeth, glad of his opponent's neat reply.

Seeing the silver cigarette case in Loris-Melikov's hand, he asked for a cigarette. And when Loris-Melikov said that they were forbidden to smoke, he winked one eye, nodding his head towards Hadji Murat's bedroom, and said that he could as long as nobody saw it. And he at once began to smoke, not inhaling and putting his red lips together awkwardly as he blew the smoke out.

"That's not good," Gamzalo said sternly, and he left the room. Khan Mahoma winked at him, too, and, while smoking, began questioning Loris-Melikov about where it was best to buy a silk beshmet and a white papakha.

"What, have you got so much money?"

"Enough," Khan Mahoma replied, winking.

"Ask him where he got his money," said Eldar, turning his handsome, smiling head to Loris.

"I won it," Khan Mahoma said quickly, and he told how, the day before, strolling about Tiflis, he had come upon a bunch of men, Russian orderlies and Armenians, playing at pitch-and-toss. The stake was big: three gold coins and many silver ones. Khan Mahoma understood at once what the game involved, and, clinking the coppers he had in his pocket, entered the circle and said he staked for all that was there.

"How could you do that? Did you have it on you?" asked Loris-Melikov.

"All I had was twelve kopecks," said Khan Mahoma, baring his teeth.

"Well, but if you'd lost?"

"There's this."

And Khan Mahoma pointed to his pistol.

"What, you'd give it to them?"

"Why give it to them? I'd have run away, and if anybody had tried to stop me, I'd have killed him. And that's that."

"And, what, you won?"

"Aya, I gathered it all up and left."

Loris-Melikov fully understood Khan Mahoma and Eldar. Khan Mahoma was a merrymaker, a carouser, who did not know what to do with his surplus of life, always cheerful, light-minded, playing with his own and other people's lives, who from that playing with life had now come over to the Russians and from that playing might in just the same way go back to Shamil tomorrow. Eldar was also fully understandable: this was a man fully devoted to his murshid, calm, strong, and firm. The only one Loris-Melikov did not understand was the red-haired Gamzalo. Loris-Melikov saw that this man was not only devoted to Shamil, but felt an insuperable loathing, scorn, disgust, and hatred for all Russians; and therefore Loris-Melikov could not understand why he had come over to the Russians. The thought sometimes occurred to Loris-Melikov, and it was shared by certain of the authorities, that Hadji Murat's coming over and his stories of enmity with Shamil were a deception, that he had come over only so as to spy out the weak spots of the Russians and, fleeing to the mountains again, to direct his forces to where the Russians were weak. And Gamzalo, with his whole being, confirmed that supposition. "The other two, and Hadji Murat himself," thought Loris-Melikov, "are able to conceal their intentions, but this one gives himself away by his unconcealed hatred."

Loris-Melikov tried to talk to him. He asked whether it was boring for him here. But, without leaving off his work, giving Loris-Melikov a sidelong glance with his one eye, he produced a hoarse and abrupt growl:

"No, it's not."

And he answered all other questions in the same way.

While Loris-Melikov was in the nukers' room, Hadji Murat's fourth murid came in, the Avar Hanefi, with his hairy face and neck and shaggy, protruding chest, as if overgrown with fur. He was an unreflecting, stalwart worker, always absorbed in what he was doing and, like Eldar, obeyed his master without argument.

When he came into the nukers' room to get rice, Loris-Melikov stopped him and asked where he was from and how long he had been with Hadji Murat.

"Five years," Hanefi replied to Loris-Melikov's question. "We're from the same aoul. My father killed his uncle, and they wanted to kill me," he said, looking calmly from under his joined eyebrows into Loris-Melikov's face. "Then I asked to be received as a brother."

"What does it mean, to be received as a brother?"

"I didn't shave my head or cut my fingernails for two months, and I came to them. They let me see Patimat, his mother. Patimat gave me her breast, and I became his brother."

In the next room the voice of Hadji Murat was heard. Eldar at once recognized his master's call and, wiping his hands, went hastily, with big strides, to the drawing room.

"He's calling you," he said, coming back. And, having given one more cigarette to the merry Khan Mahoma, Loris-Melikov went to the drawing room.

XIII

WHEN LORIS-MELIKOV CAME into the drawing room, Hadji Murat met him with a cheerful face.

"So, shall we go on?" he said, seating himself on the divan.

"Yes, certainly," said Loris-Melikov. "And I went to see your nukers and talked with them. One is a merry fellow," he added.

"Yes, Khan Mahoma is an easygoing man," said Hadji Murat.

"And I liked the young, handsome one."

"Ah, Eldar. That one's young, but firm, made of iron."

They fell silent.

"So I'll speak further?"

"Yes, yes."

"I told you how the khans were killed. Well, they killed them, and Hamzat rode to Khunzakh and sat in the khans' palace," Hadji Murat began. "There remained the mother, the khansha. Hamzat summoned her. She began to reprimand him. He winked to his murid Aselder, and he struck her from behind and killed her."

"Why should he kill her?" asked Loris-Melikov.

"What else could he do: he got his front legs over, the hind legs had to follow. The whole brood had to be finished off. And that's what they did. Shamil killed the youngest by throwing him from a cliff. All the Avars submitted to Hamzat, only my brother and I did not want to submit. We had to have his blood for the khans. We pretended to submit, but we thought only of how to have his blood. We took counsel with our grandfather and decided to wait for a moment when he left the palace and kill him from ambush. Someone overheard us, told Hamzat, and he summoned our grandfather and said: 'Watch out, if it's true your grandsons are plotting evil against me, you'll hang beside them from the same gallows. I am doing God's work, I cannot be prevented. Go and remember what I have said.' Grandfather came home and told us. Then we decided not to wait, to do the deed on the first day of the feast in the mosque. Our comrades refused—only my brother and I were left. We each took two pistols, put on our burkas, and went to the mosque. Hamzat came in with thirty murids. They were all holding drawn sabers. Beside Hamzat walked Aselder, his favorite murid—the same one who cut off the khansha's head. Seeing us, he shouted for us to take off our burkas, and came towards me. I had a dagger in my hand, and I killed him and rushed for Hamzat. But my brother Osman had already shot him. Hamzat was still alive and rushed at my brother with a dagger, but I finished him off in the head. There were about thirty murids and the two of us. They killed my brother Osman, but I fought them off, jumped out the window, and escaped. When the people learned that Hamzat had been killed, they all rose up, and the murids fled, and those who didn't were killed."

Hadji Murat paused and took a deep breath.

"That was all very well," he went on, "then it all went bad. Shamil stood in place of Hamzat. He sent envoys to me to tell me to go with him against the Russians; if I refused, he threatened to lay waste to Khunzakh and kill me. I said I wouldn't go to him and wouldn't let him come to me."

"Why didn't you go to him?" asked Loris-Melikov.

Hadji Murat frowned and did not answer at once.

"It was impossible. There was the blood of my brother Osman and of Abununtsal Khan upon Shamil. I didn't go to him. Rosen, the general, sent me an officer's rank and told me to be the commander of Avaria. All would have been well, but earlier Rosen had appointed over Avaria, first, the khan of Kazikumykh, Mahomet Mirza, and then Akhmet Khan. That one hated me. He wanted to marry his son to the khansha's daughter Saltanet. She was not given to him, and he thought it was my fault. He hated me and sent his nukers to kill me, but I escaped from them. Then he spoke against me to General Klugenau, said that I wouldn't let the Avars give firewood to the soldiers. He also told him that I had put on the turban—this one," said Hadji Murat, pointing to the turban over his papakha, "and that it meant I had gone over to Shamil. The general did not believe him and ordered him not to touch me. But when the general left for Tiflis, Akhmet Khan did it his way: he had me seized by a company of soldiers, put me in chains, and tied me to a cannon. They kept me like that for six days. On the seventh day they untied me and led me to Temir Khan Shura. I was led by forty soldiers with loaded muskets. My hands were bound, and they had orders to kill me if I tried to escape. I knew that. When we began to approach a place near Moksokh where the path was narrow and to the right there was a steep drop of about a hundred yards, I moved to the right of the soldier, to the edge of the cliff. The soldier wanted to stop me, but I jumped from the cliff and dragged the soldier with me. The soldier was battered to death, but I stayed alive. Ribs, head, arms, legs—everything was broken. I tried to crawl but couldn't. My head whirled around and I fell asleep. I woke up soaked in blood. A shepherd saw me. He called people, they took me to the aoul. Ribs and head healed, the leg healed, too, only it came out short."

And Hadji Murat stretched out his crooked leg.

"It serves me, and that's good enough," he said. "People found out and started coming to me. I recovered, moved to Tselmes. The Avars again invited me to rule over them," Hadji Murat said with calm, assured pride. "And I agreed."

Hadji Murat stood up quickly. And, taking a portfolio from a saddlebag, he drew two yellowed letters from it and handed them to Loris-Melikov. The letters were from General Klugenau. Loris-Melikov read them over. The first letter contained the following:

"Ensign Hadji Murat! You served under me—I was satisfied with you and considered you a good man. Recently Major General Akhmet Khan informed me that you are a traitor, that you have put on the turban, that you have contacts with Shamil, that you have taught the people not to listen to the Russian authorities. I ordered you arrested and delivered to me. You escaped—I do not know whether that is for better or worse, because I do not know whether you are guilty or not. Now listen to me. If your conscience is clear with regard to the great tsar, if you are not guilty of anything, come to me. Do not fear anyone—I am your defender. The khan will not do anything to you; he is my subordinate, and you have nothing to fear."

Klugenau wrote further that he had always kept his word and was just, and again admonished Hadji Murat to come over to him.

When Loris-Melikov finished the first letter, Hadji Murat took out the other letter, but before handing it to Loris-Melikov, he told him how he had answered the first letter.

"I wrote to him that I wore the turban, not for Shamil, but for the salvation of my soul, that I could not and would not go over to Shamil, because through him my father and my brothers and relations had been killed, but that neither could I come over to the Russians, because they had dishonored me. In Khunzakh, when I was bound, a certain scoundrel ——ed on me. And I cannot come over to you until that man has been killed. And above all I fear the deceitful Akhmet Khan. Then the general sent me this letter," said Hadji Murat, handing Loris-Melikov another yellowed piece of paper.

"I thank you for having answered my letter," read Loris-Melikov. "You write that you are not afraid to return, but that a dishonor inflicted on you by a certain giaour forbids it; but I assure you that Russian law is just, and before your own eyes you will see the punishment of the man who dared to insult you—I have already ordered it investigated. Listen, Hadji Murat. I have the right to be displeased with you, because you do not trust me and my honor, but I forgive you, knowing the mistrustful character of mountaineers in general. If you have a clean conscience, if you actually wear the turban for the salvation of your soul, then you are right and can boldly look me and the Russian government in the eye; and the one who dishonored you will be punished, I assure you; *your property will be returned*, and you will see and learn what Russian law is. The more so as Russians look at everything differently; in their eyes you are not harmed because some blackguard has dishonored you. I myself have allowed the Ghimrians to wear the turban, and I look upon their actions as fitting; consequently, I repeat, you have nothing to fear. Come to me with the man I am sending to you now; he is faithful to me, *he is not a slave of your enemies*, but a friend of the one who enjoys the special attention of the government."

Klugenau again went on to persuade Hadji Murat to come over.

"I didn't trust it," said Hadji Murat, when Loris-Melikov had finished the letter, "and I didn't go to Klugenau. Above all, I had to revenge myself on Akhmet Khan, and I could not do it through the Russians. Just then Akhmet Khan surrounded Tselmes and wanted to capture or kill me. I had very few men, and I was unable to fight him off. And just then a messenger came from Shamil with a letter. He promised to help me fight off Akhmet Khan and kill him, and to give me the whole of Avaria to rule over. I thought for a long time and went over to Shamil. And since then I have never ceased making war on the Russians."

Here Hadji Murat told about all his military exploits. There were a great many of them, and Loris-Melikov partly knew them. All his campaigns and raids were striking in the extraordinary swiftness of his movements and the boldness of his attacks, which were always crowned with success.

"There has never been any friendship between me and Shamil," Hadji Murat said, finishing his story, "but he feared me, and I was necessary to him. But here it so happened that I was asked who would be imam after Shamil. I said that he would be imam whose saber was sharp. This was told to Shamil, and he wanted to get rid of me. He sent me to Tabasaran. I went and took a thousand sheep and three hundred horses. But he said I had not done the right thing, and he replaced me as naïb and told me to send him all the money. I sent him a thousand pieces of gold. He sent his murids and took everything I possessed. He demanded that I come to him; I knew he wanted to kill me and did not go. He sent men to take me. I fought them off and came over to Vorontsov. Only I did not take my family. My mother, and my wife, and my son are with him. Tell the sardar: as long as my family is there, I can do nothing."

"I'll tell him," said Loris-Melikov.

"Push for it, try hard. What's mine is yours, only help me with the prince. I'm bound, and the end of the rope is in Shamil's hands."

With those words Hadji Murat finished his account to Loris-Melikov.

XIV

ON THE TWENTIETH of December Vorontsov wrote the following to the minister of war, Chernyshov. The letter was in French.[15]

"I did not write to you with the last post, my dear prince, wishing first to decide what we were going to do with Hadji Murat, and feeling myself not quite well for two or three days. In my last letter I informed you of Hadji Murat's arrival here: he came to Tiflis on the 8th; the next day I made his acquaintance, and for eight or nine days I talked with him and thought over what he might do for us later on, and especially what we are to do with him now, because he is greatly concerned about the fate of his family, and says, with all the tokens of sincerity, that as long as his family is in the hands of Shamil, he is paralyzed and unable to serve us and prove his gratitude for the friendly reception and the pardon we have granted him. The uncertainty in which he finds himself regarding the persons dear to him causes a state of feverishness in him, and the persons appointed by me to live with him here assure me that he does not sleep at night, hardly eats anything, prays constantly, and only requests permission to go riding with several Cossacks—the sole diversion and exercise possible for him, made necessary by a habit of many years. Every day he comes to me to find out if I have had any news of his family and asking me to order the gathering of all available prisoners from our various lines, so as to offer them to Shamil in exchange, to which he would add some money. There are people who will give him money for that. He keeps repeating to me: 'Save my family and then give me the chance to serve you' (best of all on the Lezghian line, in his opinion), 'and if, before the month is out, I do not render you a great service, punish me as you consider necessary.'

"I answered him that all this seems perfectly fair to me, and that many persons could be found among us who would not believe him if his family remained in the mountains, and not with us in the quality of a pledge; that I will do everything possible to gather the prisoners on our borders, and that, having no right, according to our regulations, to give him money for a ransom, in addition to what he will raise himself, I might find other means of helping him. After that I told him frankly my opinion that Shamil would in no case yield his family up to him, that he might declare it to him directly, promise him a full pardon and his former duties, threaten, if he did not return, to kill his mother, wife, and six children. I asked him if he could tell me frankly what he would do if he were to receive such a declaration from Shamil. Hadji Murat raised his eyes and hands to heaven and said that everything was in the hands of God, but that he would never give himself into the hands of his enemy, because he was fully convinced that Shamil would not forgive him and that he would not remain alive for long. For what concerns the extermination of his family, he did not think Shamil would act so light-mindedly: first, so as not to make him an enemy still more desperate and dangerous; and second, there is in Daghestan a multitude of persons, even very influential ones, who would talk him out of it. Finally, he repeated to me several times that, whatever the will of God was for the future, he was now taken up only with the thought of ransoming his family; that he beseeched me in the name of God to help him and to allow him to return to the environs of Chechnya, where, through the mediation and with the permission of our commanders, he could have contacts with his family, constant news of their actual situation and of means for freeing them; that many persons and even some naïbs in that part of enemy territory were more or less bound to him; that among all that populace already subjugated by the Russians or neutral, it would be easy for him, with our help, to have contacts very useful for achieving the goal that pursues him day and night, and the attainment of which would set him at ease and enable him to act for our benefit and earn our trust. He asks to be sent back to the Grozny fortress with an escort of twenty or thirty brave Cossacks, who would serve him as a defense against his enemies and us as a pledge of the truth of the intentions he has stated.

"You will understand, my dear prince, that for me this is all very perplexing, because, whatever I do, a great responsibility rests on me. It would be highly imprudent to trust him fully; but if we wanted to deprive him of all means of escape, we would have to lock him up, and that, in my opinion, would be both unjust and impolitic. Such a measure, news of which would quickly spread all over Daghestan, would be very damaging for us there, taking away the desire of all those (and they are many) who are prepared to go against Shamil more or less openly and who take such interest in the position with us of the bravest and most enterprising of the imam's lieutenants, who saw himself forced to give himself into our hands. The moment we treat Hadji Murat as a prisoner, the whole favorable effect of his betrayal of Shamil will be lost for us.

"Therefore I think that I could not act otherwise than I have acted, feeling, however, that I may be blamed for a great mistake, should Hadji Murat decide to escape again. In the service, and in such intricate affairs, it is difficult, not to say impossible, to follow a single straight path, without risk of being mistaken and without taking responsibility upon oneself; but once the path seems straight, one must follow it—come what may.

"I beg you, dear prince, to present it for the consideration of his majesty the sovereign emperor, and I will be happy if our august ruler deigns to approve of my action. All that I have written to you above, I have also written to Generals Zavadovsky and Kozlovsky, Kozlovsky being in direct contact with Hadji Murat, whom I have warned that without the latter's approval he is not to do anything or go anywhere. I told him that it will be even better for us if he rides out with our escort, otherwise Shamil will start trumpeting that we keep Hadji Murat locked up; but at the same time I made him promise that he would never go to Vozdvizhenskoe, because my son, to whom he first surrendered and whom he considers his kunak (friend), is not the commander of the place, and it could cause misunderstandings. Anyhow, Vozdvizhenskoe is too close to a numerous hostile populace, while for the relations he wishes to have with trusted persons, the Grozny fortress is convenient in all respects.

"Besides the twenty picked Cossacks, who, at his own request, will not move a step away from him, I have sent the cavalry captain Loris-Melikov, a worthy, excellent, and very intelligent officer, who speaks Tartar, knows Hadji Murat well, and also seems to be fully trusted by him. During the ten days which Hadji Murat spent here, incidentally, he lived in the same house as Lieutenant Colonel Prince Tarkhanov, commander of the Shushinskoe district, who was here on army business; he is a truly worthy man, and I trust him completely. He also gained the trust of Hadji Murat, and through him, since he speaks Tartar excellently, we discussed the most delicate and secret matters.

"I consulted with Tarkhanov concerning Hadji Murat, and he agreed with me completely that I had either to act as I have or to lock Hadji Murat in prison and guard him with all possible strict measures—because if we once treat him badly, he will not be easy to hold—or else he has to be removed from the territory altogether. But these last two measures would not only annul all the advantages that proceed for us from the quarrel between Hadji Murat and Shamil, but would also inevitably bring to a halt any developing murmur and possible insurrection of the mountaineers against Shamil's power. Prince Tarkhanov told me that he himself was convinced of Hadji Murat's truthfulness, and that Hadji Murat had no doubt that Shamil would never forgive him and would order him executed, despite the promised forgiveness. If there was one thing that might worry Tarkhanov in his relations with Hadji Murat, it is his attachment to his religion, and he does not conceal that Shamil could influence him from that side. But, as I have already said above, he would never convince Hadji Murat that he would not take his life either now or sometime after his return.

"That, my dear prince, is all that I wished to tell you concerning this episode in our local affairs."

XV

THIS REPORT WAS SENT from Tiflis on 24 December. On New Year's Eve, a sergeant major, having overdriven some dozen horses, and beaten some dozen coachmen until they bled, delivered it to Prince Chernyshov, then minister of war.

And on 1 January 1852, Chernyshov brought to the emperor Nicholas, among a number of other cases, this report from Vorontsov.

Chernyshov did not like Vorontsov—because of the universal respect in which he was held, and because of his enormous wealth, and because Vorontsov was a real aristocrat, while Chernyshov was, after all, a *parvenu,* and above all because of the emperor's special inclination for Vorontsov. And therefore Chernyshov profited from every occasion to harm Vorontsov as much as he could. In the previous report about Caucasian affairs, Chernyshov had managed to provoke Nicholas's displeasure with Vorontsov for the negligence of the commanders, owing to which the mountaineers had exterminated almost an entire small Caucasian detachment. Now he intended to present Vorontsov's orders about Hadji Murat from an unfavorable side. He wanted to suggest to the sovereign that Vorontsov, who always, particularly to the detriment of the Russians, protected and even indulged the natives, had acted unwisely in keeping Hadji Murat in the Caucasus; that, in all probability, Hadji Murat had come over to us only in order to spy out our means of defense, and that it would therefore be better to send Hadji Murat to the center of Russia and make use of him only when his family could be rescued from the mountains and there could be assurance of his devotion.

But this plan of Chernyshov's did not succeed, only because on that morning of 1 January, Nicholas was especially out of sorts and would not have accepted any suggestion from anyone merely out of contrariness; still less was he inclined to accept a suggestion from Chernyshov, whom he only tolerated, considering him for the time being an irreplaceable man, but, knowing of his efforts to destroy Zakhar Chernyshov during the trial of the Decembrists and his attempt to take possession of his fortune,[16] he also considered him a great scoundrel. So that, thanks to Nicholas's ill humor, Hadji Murat remained in the Caucasus, and his fate did not change, as it would have changed if Chernyshov had made his report at another time.

It was nine thirty when, in the haze of a twenty-degree frost, Chernyshov's fat, bearded coachman, in a sky-blue velvet hat with sharp peaks, sitting on the box of a small sleigh of the same sort that the emperor drove about in, pulled up to the side entrance of the Winter Palace and gave a friendly nod to his comrade, Prince Dolgoruky's coachman, who, having deposited his master, had already been standing for a long time by the porch of the palace, the reins tucked under his thickly padded behind, and rubbing his chilled hands.

Chernyshov was wearing an overcoat with a fluffy, silvery beaver collar and a three-cornered hat with cock's feathers, which went with the uniform. Throwing back the bearskin rug, he carefully freed from the sleigh his chilled feet, on which there were no galoshes (he prided himself on knowing nothing of galoshes), and briskly, with a slight jingling of spurs, walked over the carpet to the door, respectfully opened ahead of him by the doorman. In the hall, having thrown off his overcoat into the arms of an old footman, Chernyshov went to the mirror and carefully removed his hat from his curled wig. Looking himself over in the mirror, he twirled his whiskers and forelock with a habitual movement of his old man's hands, straightened his cross, aglets, and large, monogrammed epaulettes, and, stepping weakly on his badly obeying old man's legs, began to climb the carpet of the shallow stairs.

Going past the obsequiously bowing footmen who stood by the door in gala livery, Chernyshov entered the anteroom. The officer of the day, a newly appointed imperial adjutant, in a shining new uniform, epaulettes, aglets, and with a ruddy face not yet marked by dissipation, with a little black mustache and the hair of his temples brushed towards the eyes, as the emperor brushed his, met him respectfully. Prince Vassily Dolgoruky, the assistant minister of war, with a bored expression on his dull face, adorned by the same side-whiskers, mustache, and brushed-up temples as Nicholas wore, rose to meet Chernyshov and greeted him.

"*L'empereur?*" Chernyshov addressed the imperial adjutant, directing his eyes questioningly at the door of the office.

"*Sa majesté vient de rentrer,*"* said the imperial adjutant, listening to the sound of his own voice with obvious pleasure, and, stepping softly and so smoothly that a full glass of water placed on his head would not have spilled, he went up to the noiselessly opening door and, his whole being expressing reverence for the place he was entering, disappeared through it.

Dolgoruky meanwhile opened his portfolio, checking the papers that were in it.

Chernyshov, frowning, strolled about, stretching his legs and going over all that he had to report to the emperor. Chernyshov was near the door of the office when it opened again and the imperial adjutant came out, still more radiant and respectful than before, and with a gesture invited the minister and his assistant to the sovereign.

The Winter Palace had long since been rebuilt after the fire, yet Nicholas still lived on its upper floor. The office in which he received the reports of ministers and high officials was a very high-ceilinged room with four large windows. A large portrait of the emperor Alexander I hung on the main wall. Between the windows stood two desks. Along the walls several chairs, in the middle of the room an enormous writing table, at the table Nicholas's armchair and chairs for visitors.

Nicholas, in a black tunic without epaulettes, but with small shoulder straps, sat at the table, his enormous body tight-laced across the overgrown belly, and looked at the entering men with his immobile, lifeless gaze. His long, white face with its enormous, receding brow emerging from the slicked-down hair at his temples, artfully joined to the wig that covered his bald patch, was especially cold and immobile that day. His

* His Majesty has just returned.

eyes, always dull, looked duller than usual; his compressed lips under the twirled mustaches, and his fat cheeks propped on his high collar, freshly shaven, with regular, sausage-shaped side-whiskers left on them, and his chin pressed into the collar, gave his face an expression of displeasure and even of wrath. The cause of this mood was fatigue. And the cause of the fatigue was that he had been at a masked ball the night before, and, strolling as usual in his horse guards helmet with a bird on its head, among the public who either pressed towards him or timidly avoided his enormous and self-assured figure, had again met that mask who, at the last masked ball, having aroused his old man's sensuality by her whiteness, beautiful build, and tender voice, had hidden from him, promising to meet him at the next masked ball. At last night's ball she had come up to him, and he had not let her go. He had led her to the box kept in readiness especially for that purpose, where he could remain alone with his lady. Having come silently to the door of the box, Nicholas looked around, his eyes searching for the usher, but he was not there. Nicholas frowned and pushed open the door of the box himself, allowing his lady to go in first.

*"Il y a quelqu'un,"** the mask said, stopping. The box was indeed occupied. On a little velvet divan, close to each other, sat an uhlan officer and a young, pretty, blond, curly-haired woman in a domino, with her mask off. Seeing the drawn-up, towering, and wrathful figure of Nicholas, the blond woman hastily covered herself with the mask, and the uhlan officer, dumbfounded with terror, not getting up from the divan, stared at Nicholas with fixed eyes.

Accustomed though Nicholas was to the terror he aroused in people, that terror had always been pleasing to him, and he liked on occasion to astound the people thrown into terror, addressing them by contrast with affable words. And so he did now.

"Well, brother, you're a bit younger than I," he said to the officer numb with terror, "you might yield the place to me."

The officer leaped up and, turning pale, then red, cowering, silently followed the mask out of the box, and Nicholas was left alone with his lady.

The mask turned out to be a pretty, innocent, twenty-year-old girl,

* There's somebody here.

the daughter of a Swedish governess. The girl told Nicholas how, when still a child, she had fallen in love with him from his portraits, had idolized him, and had resolved to win his attention at any cost. And now she had won it, and, as she said, she wanted nothing more. The girl was taken to the usual place for Nicholas's meetings with women, and Nicholas spent more than an hour with her.

When he returned to his room that night and lay down on the narrow, hard bed, which he took pride in, and covered himself with his cloak, which he considered (and he said so) as famous as Napoleon's hat, he could not fall asleep for a long time. He recalled now the frightened and rapturous expression of the girl's white face, now the powerful, full shoulders of his usual mistress, Mme Nelidov, and drew comparisons between the one and the other. That debauchery was not a good thing in a married man did not even occur to him, and he would have been very surprised if anyone had condemned him for it. But, even though he was convinced that he had acted as he ought, he was left with some sort of unpleasant aftertaste, and, to stifle that feeling, he began thinking about something that always soothed him: about what a great man he was.

Even though he had fallen asleep late, he got up before eight o'clock, as always, and, having performed his usual toilette, having rubbed his big, well-fed body with ice and prayed to God, he recited the usual prayers he had been saying since childhood—the Hail Mary, the Creed, the Our Father—without ascribing any significance to the words he pronounced, and went out through the side entrance to the embankment, in an overcoat and a peaked cap.

Midway along the embankment, he met a student from the law school, as enormously tall as himself, in a uniform and hat. Seeing the uniform of the school, which he disliked for its freethinking, Nicholas frowned, but the tallness of the student, the zealous way he stood to attention and saluted with a deliberately thrust-out elbow, softened his displeasure.

"What is your name?" he asked.

"Polosatov, Your Imperial Majesty!"

"Fine fellow!"

The student went on standing with his hand to his hat. Nicholas stopped.

"Want to join the army?"

"No, sir, Your Imperial Majesty."

"Blockhead!" and Nicholas, turning away, walked on and began loudly uttering the first words that came to him. "Koperwein, Koperwein," he repeated several times the name of last night's girl. "Nasty, nasty." He was not thinking of what he was saying, but stifled his feeling by concentrating on the words. "Yes, what would Russia be without me?" he said to himself, again sensing the approach of the unpleasant feeling. "Yes, what would, not just Russia, but Europe be without me?" And he remembered his brother-in-law, the king of Prussia, and his weakness and stupidity, and shook his head.

Going back to the porch, he saw the carriage of Elena Pavlovna, with a handsome footman, driving up to the Saltykov entrance. Elena Pavlovna was for him the personification of those empty people who talked not only about science and poetry, but also about governing people, imagining that they could govern themselves better than he, Nicholas, governed them. He knew that, however much he quashed these people, they surfaced again and again. And he recalled his recently deceased brother, Mikhail Pavlovich. And a feeling of vexation and sadness came over him. He frowned gloomily and again began whispering the first words that came to him. He stopped whispering only when he entered the palace. Going into his apartments and smoothing his side-whiskers and the hair on his temples and the hairpiece on his bald patch before the mirror, he twirled his mustaches and went straight to the office where reports were received.

He received Chernyshov first. By Nicholas's face, and mainly by his eyes, Chernyshov understood at once that he was especially out of sorts that day, and, knowing of his adventure the night before, he understood the cause of it. Having greeted Chernyshov coldly and invited him to be seated, Nicholas fixed his lifeless eyes on him.

The first business in Chernyshov's report was a case of theft discovered among commissary officials; then there was the matter of a transfer of troops on the Prussian border; then the nomination for New Year awards of certain persons omitted from the first list; then there was the dispatch from Vorontsov about Hadji Murat's coming over; and, finally, an unpleasant case of a student in the medical academy who had made an attempt on a professor's life.

Nicholas, with silently compressed lips, stroked the sheets of paper with his big white hands, with a gold ring on one ring finger, and listened to the report about the theft, not taking his eyes from Chernyshov's forehead and forelock.

Nicholas was convinced that everyone stole. He knew that the commissary officials now had to be punished and decided to send them all as soldiers, but he also knew that that would not prevent those who filled the vacated posts from doing the same thing. It was in the nature of officials to steal, and his duty was to punish them, and sick of it as he was, he conscientiously performed his duty.

"It seems there's only one honest man in our Russia," he said.

Chernyshov understood at once that this only man in Russia was Nicholas himself, and he smiled approvingly.

"Surely, that's so, Your Majesty," he said.

"Leave it, I'll write my decision," said Nicholas, taking the paper and placing it on the left side of the table.

After that, Chernyshov started reporting about awards and the troop transfer. Nicholas glanced through the list, crossed out several names, and then briefly and resolutely ordered the transfer of two divisions to the Prussian border.

Nicholas could never forgive the Prussian king for granting his people a constitution after the year forty-eight, and therefore, while expressing the most friendly feelings for his brother-in-law in letters and words, he considered it necessary to keep troops on the Prussian border just in case. These troops might also prove necessary so that, in case of a popular insurrection in Prussia (Nicholas saw a readiness for insurrection everywhere), they could be sent to defend his brother-in-law's throne, as he had sent troops to defend Austria against the Hungarians. These troops on the border were also needed to give more weight and significance to his advice to the Prussian king.

"Yes, what would happen to Russia now, if it weren't for me?" he thought again.

"Well, what else?" he said.

"A sergeant major from the Caucasus," said Chernyshov, and he began to report what Vorontsov had written about Hadji Murat's coming over.

"Really," said Nicholas. "A good beginning."

"Obviously the plan worked out by Your Majesty is beginning to bear fruit," said Chernyshov.

This praise of his strategic abilities was especially pleasing to Nicholas, because, though he was proud of his strategic abilities, at the bottom of his heart he was aware that he had none. And now he wanted to hear more detailed praise of himself.

"How do you mean?" he asked.

"I mean that if we had long ago followed Your Majesty's plan—moving forward gradually, though slowly, cutting down forests, destroying provisions—the Caucasus would have been subjugated long ago. Hadji Murat's coming over I put down only to that. He realized that it was no longer possible for them to hold out."

"True," said Nicholas.

Despite the fact that the plan of a slow movement into enemy territory by means of cutting down forests and destroying provisions was the plan of Ermolov and Velyaminov, and the complete opposite of Nicholas's plan, according to which it was necessary to take over Shamil's residence at once and devastate that nest of robbers, and according to which the Dargo expedition of 1845 had been undertaken, at the cost of so many human lives—despite that, Nicholas also ascribed to himself the plan of slow movement, the progressive cutting down of forests, and the destruction of provisions. It would seem that, in order to believe that the plan of slow movement, the cutting down of forests, and the destruction of provisions was his plan, it would be necessary to conceal the fact that he had precisely insisted on the completely opposite military undertaking of the year forty-five. But he did not conceal it and was proud both of his plan of the expedition of the year forty-five and of the plan of slow movement forward, despite the fact that these two plans obviously contradicted each other. The constant, obvious flattery, contrary to all evidence, of the people around him had brought him to the point that he no longer saw his contradictions, no longer conformed his actions and words to reality, logic, or even simple common sense, but was fully convinced that all his orders, however senseless, unjust, and inconsistent with each other, became sensible, just, and consistent with each other only because he gave them.

Such, too, was his decision about the student of the medico-surgical academy, about whom Chernyshov began to report after the report on the Caucasus.

What had happened was that a young man who had twice failed his examinations was taking them for the third time, and when the examiner again did not pass him, the morbidly nervous student, seeing injustice in it, seized a penknife from the desk and, in something like a fit of frenzy, fell upon the professor and inflicted several insignificant wounds.

"What is his last name?" asked Nicholas.

"Bzhezovsky."

"A Pole?"

"Of Polish origin and a Catholic," replied Chernyshov.

Nicholas frowned.

He had done much evil to the Poles. To explain that evil he had to be convinced that all Poles were scoundrels. And Nicholas regarded them as such and hated them in proportion to the evil he had done them.

"Wait a little," he said and, closing his eyes, he lowered his head.

Chernyshov knew, having heard it more than once from Nicholas, that whenever he had to decide some important question, he had only to concentrate for a few moments and inspiration would come to him, and the most correct decision would take shape by itself, as if some inner voice told him what had to be done. He now thought about how he could more fully satisfy that feeling of spite against the Poles that had been aroused in him by the story of this student, and his inner voice prompted him to the following decision. He took the report and wrote on its margin in his large hand: *"Deserves the death penalty. But, thank God, we do not have the death penalty. And it is not for me to introduce it. Have him run the gauntlet of a thousand men twelve times. Nicholas"*—he signed with his unnatural, enormous flourish.

Nicholas knew that twelve thousand rods was not only a certain, painful death, but also excessive cruelty, because five thousand strokes were enough to kill the strongest man. But it pleased him to be implacably cruel and pleased him to think that we had no death penalty.

Having written his decision about the student, he moved it over to Chernyshov.

"Here," he said. "Read it."

Chernyshov read it and, as a sign of respectful astonishment at the wisdom of the decision, inclined his head.

"And have all the students brought to the square, so that they can be present at the punishment," Nicholas added.

"It will do them good. I'll destroy this revolutionary spirit, I'll tear it up by the roots," he thought.

"Yes, Sire," said Chernyshov and, after a pause, he straightened his forelock and went back to the Caucasian report.

"What, then, do you order me to write to Mikhail Semyonovich?"

"To adhere firmly to my system of laying waste to habitations, destroying provisions in Chechnya, and harrying them with raids," said Nicholas.

"What are your orders about Hadji Murat?" asked Chernyshov.

"Why, Vorontsov writes that he wants to make use of him in the Caucasus."

"Isn't that risky?" said Chernyshov, avoiding Nicholas's eyes. "I'm afraid Mikhail Semyonovich is too trusting."

"And what would you think?" Nicholas asked sharply, noticing Chernyshov's intention to present Vorontsov's orders in a bad light.

"I would think it's safer to send him to Russia."

"You think so," Nicholas said mockingly. "But I do not think so and agree with Vorontsov. Write that to him."

"Yes, Sire," said Chernyshov and, standing up, he began taking his leave.

Dolgoruky also took his leave. In the whole time of the report, he had said only a few words about the transfer of troops, in answer to Nicholas's questions.

After Chernyshov, the governor general of the western provinces, Bibikov, was received, having come to take his leave. Approving of the measures Bibikov had taken against the rebellious peasants, who did not want to convert to Orthodoxy,[17] he told him to try all the disobedient in military court. That meant sentencing them to run the gauntlet. Besides that, he ordered the editor of a newspaper to be sent as a soldier for publishing information about the reregistering of several thousand state peasants as crown peasants.

"I do this because I consider it necessary," he said. "And I allow no discussion of it."

Bibikov understood all the cruelty of the order about the Uniates and all the injustice of the transfer of state peasants, that is, the only free ones at that time, to the crown, that is, making them serfs of the tsar's family. But it was impossible to object. To disagree with Nicholas's orders meant to lose all that brilliant position which he now enjoyed, and which he had spent forty years acquiring. And therefore he humbly bowed his dark, graying head in a sign of submission and readiness to carry out the cruel, insane, and dishonest supreme will.

After dismissing Bibikov, Nicholas, with a consciousness of duty well done, stretched, glanced at the clock, and went to dress for his coming out. Having put on his uniform with epaulettes, decorations, and a sash, he went out to the reception halls, where more than a hundred men in uniform and women in low-cut fancy dresses, all standing in assigned places, waited tremblingly for his coming out.

With his lifeless gaze, with his thrust-out chest and his tight-laced belly protruding from the lacing above and below, he came out to these waiting people, and, feeling that all eyes were directed at him with trembling obsequiousness, he assumed a still more solemn air. When he met the eyes of familiar persons, remembering who was who, he stopped and said a few words, sometimes in Russian, sometimes in French, and, piercing them with his cold, lifeless gaze, listened to what they said to him.

Having received their felicitations, Nicholas went on to church.

God, through his servants, greeted and praised Nicholas, just as the secular people had done, and he, though he found it tedious, received those greetings and praises as his due. All this had to be so, because on him depended the welfare and happiness of the whole world, and though it wearied him, he still did not deny the world his assistance. When, at the end of the liturgy, the magnificent deacon, his long hair combed loose, proclaimed "Many Years,"[18] and with beautiful voices the choristers all as one took up these words, Nicholas glanced behind him and noticed Mme Nelidov with her splendid shoulders, and decided the comparison with last night's girl in her favor.

After the liturgy he went to the empress and spent several minutes in the family circle, joking with his children and wife. Then he went through the Hermitage to see the minister of court Volkonsky and, among other things, charged him with paying an annual pension out of special funds to the mother of last night's girl. And from him he went for his usual promenade.

Dinner that day was in the Pompeian Hall. Besides the younger sons, Nicholas and Mikhail, there were also invited Baron Liven, Count Rzhevussky, Dolgoruky, the Prussian ambassador, and the Prussian king's adjutant general.

While waiting for the empress and emperor to come out, an interesting conversation began between the Prussian ambassador and Baron Liven to do with the latest alarming news from Poland.

"La Pologne et le Caucase, ce sont les deux cautères de la Russie," said Liven. *"Il nous faut cent mille hommes à peu près dans chacun de ces deux pays."**

The ambassador expressed feigned surprise that it was so.

"Vous dites la Pologne,"† he said.

"Oh, oui, c'était un coup de maître de Metternich de nous en avoir laissé l'embarras . . ."‡

At this point in the conversation the empress came in with her shaking head and frozen smile, and Nicholas behind her.

At the table Nicholas told them about Hadji Murat's coming over and said that the war in the Caucasus should end soon as the result of his order about restricting the mountaineers by cutting down the forests and his system of fortifications.

The ambassador, having exchanged fleeting glances with the Prussian adjutant general, with whom he had spoken that morning about Nicholas's unfortunate weakness of considering himself a great strategist, highly praised this plan, which proved once again Nicholas's great strategic abilities.

After dinner Nicholas went to the ballet, where hundreds of bare women marched about in tights. One especially caught his eye and, summoning the ballet master, Nicholas thanked him and ordered that he be given a diamond ring.

The next day, during Chernyshov's report, Nicholas confirmed once more his instructions to Vorontsov, that now, since Hadji Murat had come over, they should intensify the harrying of Chechnya and hem it in with a cordon line.

Chernyshov wrote in that sense to Vorontsov, and the next day another sergeant major, overdriving the horses and beating the coachmen's faces, galloped off to Tiflis.

* Poland and the Caucasus are the two running sores of Russia . . . We need about a hundred thousand men in each of the two countries.

† Poland, you say.

‡ Oh, yes, it was a masterstroke of Metternich's to have left us the inconvenience of it . . .

XVI

In fulfillment of these instructions from Nicholas, a raid into Chechnya was undertaken at once, in January 1852.

The detachment sent on the raid consisted of four infantry battalions, two hundred Cossacks, and eight guns. The column marched along the road. On both sides of the column, in an unbroken line, descending into and climbing out of the gullies, marched chasseurs in high boots, fur jackets, and papakhas, with muskets on their shoulders and cartridges in bandoliers. As always, the detachment moved through enemy territory keeping as silent as possible. Only the guns clanked now and then, jolting over ditches, or an artillery horse, not understanding the order for silence, snorted or neighed, or an angered commander yelled in a hoarse, restrained voice at his subordinates because the line was too strung out, or moved too close or too far from the column. Only once the silence was broken by a she-goat with a white belly and rump and a gray back and a similar billy goat with short, back-bent horns, who leaped from a small bramble patch between the line and the column. The beautiful, frightened animals, making big leaps and tucking up their front legs, came flying so close to the column that some of the soldiers ran after them with shouts and guffaws, intending to stick them with their bayonets, but the goats turned back, leaped through the line, and, pursued by several horsemen and the company dogs, sped off like birds into the mountains.

It was still winter, but the sun was beginning to climb higher, and by noon, when the detachment, which had set off early in the morning, had already gone some seven miles, it had warmed up so much that the men felt hot, and its rays were so bright that it was painful to look at the steel of the bayonets and the gleams that suddenly flashed on the bronze of the cannons like little suns.

Behind was the swift, clear river the detachment had just crossed, ahead were cultivated fields and meadows with shallow gullies, further ahead the mysterious, dark hills covered with forest, beyond the dark hills crags jutting up, and on the high horizon—eternally enchanting, eternally changing, playing in the light like diamonds—the snowy mountains.

At the head of the fifth company, in a black tunic, a papakha, and with a saber across his shoulder, marched the tall, handsome officer Butler, recently transferred from the guards, experiencing a vigorous feeling of the joy of life, and at the same time of the danger of death, and the desire for activity, and the consciousness of belonging to an enormous whole governed by a single will. Today Butler was going into action for the second time, and it was a joy to him to think that they were about to be fired at, and that he not only would not duck his head as a cannonball flew over or pay attention to the whistle of bullets, but would carry his head high, as he had done already, and look about at his comrades and soldiers with a smile in his eyes, and start talking in the most indifferent voice about something irrelevant.

The detachment turned off the good road and onto a little-used one, crossing a harvested cornfield, and was just approaching the forest, when—no one could see from where—a cannonball flew over with a sinister whistle and landed at the middle of the baggage train, by the road, in the cornfield, throwing up dirt.

"It's beginning," Butler said, smiling merrily, to a comrade walking next to him.

And indeed, after the cannonball, a dense crowd of Chechen horsemen with standards appeared from the forest. In the middle of the party was a large green standard, and the old sergeant major of the company, who was very long-sighted, informed the nearsighted Butler that it must be Shamil himself. The party descended the hill and appeared on the crest of the nearest gully to the right and began to descend into it. A little general in a warm black tunic and a papakha with a big white lambskin top rode up to Butler's company on his ambler and ordered him to go to the right against the descending horsemen. Butler quickly led his company in the direction indicated, but before he had time to descend into the gully, he heard two cannon shots behind him, one after the other. He looked back: two clouds of blue-gray smoke rose above the two cannon and stretched out along the gully. The party, obviously not expecting artillery, went back. Butler's company began to fire after the mountaineers, and the whole hollow became covered with powder smoke. Only above the hollow could the mountaineers be seen, hastily retreating and returning the fire of the pursuing Cossacks. The detachment went on after the mountaineers, and on the slope of a second gully an aoul appeared.

Butler and his company, following the Cossacks, came running into the aoul. There were no inhabitants. The soldiers had been ordered to burn grain, hay, and the saklyas themselves. Pungent smoke spread over the whole aoul, and in this smoke soldiers poked about, dragging out of the saklyas whatever they could find, and mainly catching and shooting the chickens that the mountaineers could not take with them. The officers sat down away from the smoke and had lunch and drank. The sergeant major brought them several honeycombs on a board. There was no sign of the Chechens. A little past noon came the order to retreat. The companies formed a column beyond the aoul, and Butler ended up in the rear guard. As soon as they set off, Chechens appeared and, riding after the detachment, escorted it with gunfire.

When the detachment came out into the open, the mountaineers dropped behind. None of Butler's men was wounded, and he went back in the most merry and cheerful spirits.

When the detachment, having waded back across the little river they had crossed that morning, stretched out over the cornfields and meadows, singers stepped forward by company and songs rang out. There was no wind, the air was fresh, clean, and so transparent that the snowy mountains, which were some seventy miles away, seemed very close, and when the singers fell silent, the measured tramp of feet and clank of guns could be heard, as a background against which the songs started and stopped. The song sung in Butler's fifth company had been composed by a junker for the glory of the regiment and was sung to a dance tune with the refrain: "What can compare, what can compare, with the chasseurs, with the chasseurs!"

Butler rode beside his next in command, Major Petrov, with whom he lived, and could not rejoice enough at his decision to leave the guards and go to the Caucasus. The main reason for his transfer from the guards was that in Petersburg he had lost so much at cards that he had nothing left. He was afraid that he would not be able to keep from gambling if he stayed in the guards, and he had nothing to gamble with. Now it was all over. This was a different life, and such a fine, dashing one! He forgot now about his ruin and his unpaid debts. And the Caucasus, the war, the soldiers, the officers, the drunken and good-natured, brave Major Petrov—all this seemed so good to him that he sometimes could not believe he was not in Petersburg, not in smoke-filled rooms bending corners and punting, hating the banker and feeling an oppressive ache in his head, but here in this wonderful country, among the dashing Caucasians.

"What can compare, what can compare, with the chasseurs, with the chasseurs!" sang his singers. His horse went merrily in step with this music. The shaggy gray company dog Trezorka, like a commander, its tail curled up, ran ahead of Butler's company with a preoccupied air. At heart Butler felt cheerful, calm, and merry. War presented itself to him only as a matter of subjecting himself to danger, to the possibility of death, and thereby earning awards, and the respect of his comrades here and of his friends in Russia. The other side of war—the death, the wounds of soldiers, officers, mountaineers—strange as it is to say, did not present itself to his imagination. Unconsciously, to preserve his poetic notion of war, he never even looked at the killed and wounded. And so it was now: we had three men killed and twelve wounded. He passed by a corpse lying on its back, and saw with only one eye the strange position of the waxen arm and the dark red spot on the head, and did not stop to look. The mountaineers presented themselves to him only as dzhigit horsemen from whom one had to defend oneself.

"So it goes, old boy," the major said between songs. "Not like with you in Petersburg: dress right, dress left. We do our work and go home. Mashurka will serve us a pie, some nice cabbage soup. That's life! Right? Now, lads, 'As Dawn Was Breaking,' " he ordered his favorite song.

The major lived maritally with the daughter of a surgeon's assistant, first known as Mashka, and then as Marya Dmitrievna. Marya Dmitrievna was a beautiful, fair-haired, thirty-year-old, childless woman, all covered with freckles. Whatever her past had been, she was now the major's faithful companion, took care of him like a nurse, and the major needed it, because he often drank himself into oblivion.

When they reached the fortress, it was all as the major had foreseen. Marya Dmitrievna fed him and Butler and two other invited officers of the detachment a nourishing, tasty dinner, and the major ate and drank so much that he could not speak and went to his room to sleep. Butler, likewise tired, but pleased and slightly tipsy from too much chikhir, went to his room, and having barely managed to undress, put his hand under his handsome curly head, and fell fast asleep, without dreaming or waking up.

XVII

THE AOUL DEVASTATED by the raid was the one in which Hadji Murat had spent the night before his coming over to the Russians.

Sado, with whom Hadji Murat had stayed, was leaving for the mountains with his family when the Russians approached the aoul. When he came back to his aoul, he found his saklya destroyed: the roof had fallen in, the door and posts of the little gallery were burned down, and the inside was befouled. His son, the handsome boy with shining eyes who had looked rapturously at Hadji Murat, was brought dead to the mosque on a horse covered by a burka. He had been stabbed in the back with a bayonet. The fine-looking woman who had waited on Hadji Murat during his visit, now, in a smock torn in front, revealing her old, sagging breasts, and with her hair undone, stood over her son and clawed her face until it bled and wailed without ceasing. Sado took a pick and shovel and went with some relations to dig a grave for his son. The old grandfather sat by the wall of the destroyed saklya and, whittling a little stick, stared dully before him. He had just come back from his apiary. The two haystacks formerly there had been burned; the apricot and cherry trees he had planted and nursed were broken and scorched and, worst of all, the beehives had all been burned. The wailing of women could be heard in all the houses and on the square, where two more bodies had been brought. The small children wailed along with their mothers. Hungry cattle, who had nothing to eat, also bellowed. The older children did not play, but looked at their elders with frightened eyes.

The spring had been befouled, obviously on purpose, so that it was impossible to take water from it. The mosque was also befouled, and the mullah and his assistants were cleaning it up.

The old heads of households gathered on the square and, squatting down, discussed their situation. Of hatred for the Russians no one even spoke. The feeling that was experienced by all the Chechens, big and small, was stronger than hatred. It was not hatred, but a refusal to recognize these Russian dogs as human beings, and such loathing, disgust, and bewilderment before the absurd cruelty of these beings, that the wish to exterminate them, like the wish to exterminate rats, venomous spiders, and wolves, was as natural as the sense of self-preservation.

The inhabitants were faced with a choice: to stay where they were and restore with terrible effort all that had been established with such labor and had been so easily and senselessly destroyed, and to expect at any moment a repetition of the same, or, contrary to religious law and their loathing and contempt for them, to submit to the Russians.

The old men prayed and unanimously decided to send envoys to Shamil asking him for help, and at once set about restoring what had been destroyed.

XVIII

ON THE THIRD DAY after the raid, Butler, not very early in the morning, went out by the back door, intending to stroll and have a breath of air before morning tea, which he usually took together with Petrov. The sun had already come out from behind the mountains, and it hurt to look at the white daub cottages lit up by it on the right side of the street, but then, as always, it was cheering and soothing to look to the left, at the receding and rising black hills covered with forest, and at the opaque line of snowy mountains visible beyond the gorge, trying, as always, to simulate clouds.

Butler looked at these mountains, breathed with all his lungs, and rejoiced that he was alive, and that precisely he was alive, and in this beautiful world. He also rejoiced a little at having borne himself so well in action yesterday, both during the attack and, especially, during the retreat, when things got rather hot; rejoiced, too, remembering how, in the evening, on their return from the sortie, Masha, or Marya Dmitrievna, Petrov's companion, had fed them and had been especially simple and nice with them all, but in particular, as he thought, had been affectionate to him. Marya Dmitrievna, with her thick braid, broad shoulders, high bosom, and the beaming smile of her kindly, freckled face, involuntarily attracted Butler, as a strong, young, unmarried man, and it even seemed to him that she desired him. But he reckoned that it would be a bad way to treat a kind, simple-hearted comrade, and he maintained a most simple, respectful attitude towards Marya Dmitrievna, and was glad of it in himself. He was just now thinking of that.

His thoughts were distracted when he heard in front of him the rapid beat of many horses' hooves on the dusty road, as of several men galloping. He raised his head and saw at the end of the street a small group of horsemen approaching at a walk. Ahead of some twenty Cossacks, two men were riding: one in a white cherkeska and a tall papakha with a turban, the other an officer in the Russian service, dark, hook-nosed, in a blue cherkeska with an abundance of silver on his clothes and weapons. Under the horseman in the turban was a handsome light-maned chestnut stallion with a small head and beautiful eyes; under the officer was a tall, showy Karabakh horse. Butler, a horse fancier, at once appraised the vigorous strength of the first horse and stopped to find out who these people were. The officer addressed Butler:

"This army commander house?" he asked, betraying his non-Russian origin both by his ungrammatical speech and by his pronunciation, and pointing his whip at Ivan Matveevich's house.

"The very one," said Butler. "And who's that?" he asked, coming closer to the officer and indicating the man in the turban with his eyes.

"That Hadji Murat. Come here, stay with army commander," said the officer.

Butler knew about Hadji Murat and his coming over to the Russians, but he had never expected to see him here in this little stronghold.

Hadji Murat was looking at him amicably.

"Greetings, *koshkoldy,*" he said the Tartar greeting he had learned.

"*Saubul,*" replied Hadji Murat, nodding his head. He rode up to Butler and gave him his hand, from two fingers of which hung a whip.

"The commander?" he asked.

"No, the commander's here, I'll go and call him," said Butler, addressing the officer and going up the steps and pushing at the door.

But the door of the "main entrance," as Marya Dmitrievna called it, was locked. Butler knocked, but, receiving no answer, went around to the back door. Having called his orderly and received no answer, and not finding either of his two orderlies, he went to the kitchen. Marya Dmitrievna, flushed, a kerchief on her head and her sleeves rolled up on her plump white arms, was cutting rolled-out dough, as white as her arms, into pieces for little pies.

"Where are the orderlies?" asked Butler.

"Getting drunk somewhere," said Marya Dmitrievna. "What do you want?"

"To open the door. You've got a whole crowd of mountaineers in front of your house. Hadji Murat has come."

"Tell me another one," said Marya Dmitrievna, smiling.

"I'm not joking. It's true. They're standing by the porch."

"Can it be?" said Marya Dmitrievna.

"Why should I make it up? Go and look, they're standing by the porch."

"That's a surprise," said Marya Dmitrievna, rolling down her sleeves and feeling with her hand for the pins in her thick braid. "Then I'll go and wake up Ivan Matveevich," she said.

"No, I'll go myself. And you, Bondarenko, go and open the door," said Butler.

"Well, that's good enough," said Marya Dmitrievna, and she went back to what she was doing.

On learning that Hadji Murat had come to him, Ivan Matveevich, who had already heard that Hadji Murat was in the Grozny fortress, was not surprised by it in the least, but got up, rolled a cigarette, lit it, and began to dress, clearing his throat loudly and grumbling at the superiors who had sent "this devil" to him. Having dressed, he asked his orderly for "medicine." And the orderly, knowing that "medicine" meant vodka, brought it to him.

"There's nothing worse than mixing," he grumbled, drinking up the vodka and taking a bite of black bread. "I drank chikhir yesterday, so today I've got a headache. Well, now I'm ready," he finished and went to the drawing room, where Butler had already brought Hadji Murat and the officer who accompanied him.

The officer escorting Hadji Murat handed Ivan Matveevich the order of the commander of the left flank to receive Hadji Murat, to allow him to have communications with the mountaineers through scouts, but by no means to let him leave the fortress otherwise than with a Cossack escort.

After reading the paper, Ivan Matveevich looked intently at Hadji Murat and again began to scrutinize the paper. Having shifted his eyes from the paper to his guest several times like that, he finally rested his eyes on Hadji Murat and said:

"*Yakshi, bek-yakshi.* Let him stay. But tell him I've been ordered not to let him leave. And orders are sacred. And we'll put him up—what do you think, Butler—shall we put him up in the office?"

Before Butler had time to reply, Marya Dmitrievna, who had come from the kitchen and was standing in the doorway, addressed Ivan Matveevich:

"Why in the office? Put him up here. We'll give him the guest room and the storeroom. At least we can keep an eye on him," she said and, glancing at Hadji Murat and meeting his eyes, she hastily turned away.

"You know, I think Marya Dmitrievna is right," said Butler.

"Well, well, off with you, women have no business here," Ivan Matveevich said, frowning.

Throughout the conversation, Hadji Murat sat, his hand tucked behind the hilt of his dagger, smiling somewhat scornfully. He said it made no difference to him where he lived. One thing that he needed and that the sardar had permitted him was to have contacts with the mountaineers, and therefore he wished that they be allowed to come to him. Ivan Matveevich said that that would be done, and asked Butler to entertain the guests until they were brought a bite to eat and their rooms were prepared, while he went to the office to write out the necessary papers and give the necessary orders.

Hadji Murat's relations with his new acquaintances were at once defined very clearly. From their first acquaintance Hadji Murat felt loathing and contempt for Ivan Matveevich and always treated him haughtily. To Marya Dmitrievna, who prepared and brought his food, he took a special liking. He liked her simplicity, and the special beauty of a nationality foreign to him, and the attraction she felt to him, which she transmitted to him unconsciously. He tried not to look at her, not to speak with her, but his eyes involuntarily turned to her and followed her movements.

With Butler he became friendly at once, from their first acquaintance, and talked with him much and eagerly, questioning him about his life and telling him about his own and passing on the news brought to him by the scouts about the situation of his family, and even consulting with him about what to do.

The news conveyed to him by the scouts was not good. During the four days he had spent in the fortress, they had come to him twice, and both times the news had been bad.

XIX

Soon after Hadji Murat came over to the Russians, his family was brought to the aoul of Vedeno and was kept there under watch, waiting for Shamil's decision. The women—old Patimat and Hadji Murat's two wives—and their five small children lived under guard in the saklya of the lieutenant Ibrahim Rashid, but Hadji Murat's son, the eighteen-year-old boy Yusuf, sat in prison, that is, in a hole more than seven feet deep, together with four criminals awaiting, like him, the deciding of their fate.

The decision did not come, because Shamil was away. He was on campaign against the Russians.

On 6 January 1852, Shamil was returning home to Vedeno after a battle with the Russians in which, according to the opinion of the Russians, he had been crushed and had fled to Vedeno, while according to his own opinion and that of all the murids, he had been victorious and had routed the Russians. In this battle—something that happened very rarely—he himself had fired his rifle and, snatching out his saber, had sent his horse straight at the Russians, but the murids accompanying him had held him back. Two of them had been killed right beside Shamil.

It was midday when Shamil, surrounded by the party of murids, caracoling around him, firing off their rifles and pistols, and ceaselessly singing *"La ilaha il Allah,"* rode up to his place of residence.

All the people of the large aoul of Vedeno were standing in the street and on the roofs to meet their ruler, and in a sign of festivity also fired off their muskets and pistols. Shamil rode on a white Arabian stallion, who merrily tugged at the reins as they neared home. The horse's attire was of the most simple, without gold or silver ornaments: a finely worked red leather bridle with a groove down the middle, cup-shaped metal stirrups, and a red blanket showing from under the saddle. The imam was wearing a fur-lined brown broadcloth coat, with black fur showing at the collar and cuffs, tightly girded around his slender and long body by a black belt with a dagger hung from it. On his head was a tall papakha with a flat top and a black tassel, wrapped with a white turban, the end of which hung down behind his neck. On his feet were soft green chuviaki, on his calves tight black leggings trimmed with simple cord.

In general there was nothing on the imam that glittered, gold or silver, and his tall, straight, powerful figure, in unadorned clothes, surrounded by murids with gold and silver ornaments on their clothes and weapons, produced that very impression of grandeur that he wanted and knew how to produce in people. His pale face, framed by a trimmed red beard, with its constantly narrowed little eyes, was perfectly immobile, like stone. As he rode through the aoul, he felt thousands of eyes directed at him, but his eyes did not look at anyone. The wives of Hadji Murat and their children, together with all the inhabitants of the saklya, also came out to the gallery to watch the imam's entrance. Only old Patimat, Hadji Murat's mother, did not come out, but remained sitting as she had been sitting, with disheveled gray hair, on the floor of the saklya, clasping her thin knees with her long arms, and, blinking her jet-black eyes, watched the burning-down logs in the fireplace. She, like her son, had always hated Shamil, now more than ever, and she did not want to see him.

Neither did Hadji Murat's son see the triumphal entry of Shamil. He only heard the singing and shooting from his dark, stinking hole, and suffered as only young people full of life suffer deprived of freedom. Sitting in the stinking hole and seeing all the same unfortunate, dirty, exhausted people imprisoned with him, for the most part hating each other, he was passionately envious of those who, enjoying air, light, freedom, were now caracoling on spirited horses around the ruler, shooting and singing as one: *"La ilaha il Allah."*

Having passed through the aoul, Shamil rode into a big courtyard, adjoining an inner one in which Shamil's seraglio was located. Two armed Lezghians met Shamil by the open gates of the first courtyard. This courtyard was filled with people. There were some who had come from distant places on their own business, there were petitioners, there were those summoned by Shamil himself for trial and sentencing. At Shamil's entry, all those who were in the courtyard rose and respectfully greeted the imam, putting their hands to their chests. Some knelt and stayed that way all the while Shamil was riding across the courtyard from the one, outside, gate to the other, inner one. Though Shamil recognized among those waiting many persons who were displeasing to him and many tedious petitioners demanding to be attended to, he rode past them with the same unchanging, stony face, and, riding into the inner courtyard, dismounted at the gallery of his lodgings, to the left of the gate.

After the strain of the campaign, not so much physical as spiritual, because Shamil, despite the public recognition of his campaign as victorious, knew that his campaign had been a failure, that many Chechen aouls had been burned and laid waste, and the changeable, light-minded Chechen people were wavering, and some of them, nearest to the Russians, were now ready to go over to them—all this was difficult, measures had to be taken against it, yet at that moment Shamil did not want to do anything, did not want to think about anything. He now wanted only one thing: rest and the delight of the familial caresses of his favorite among his wives, Aminet, the eighteen-year-old, dark-eyed, swift-footed Kist.

But not only was it impossible even to think now of seeing Aminet, who was right there behind the fence in the inner courtyard that separated the wives' lodgings from the men's (Shamil was even sure that now, as he was getting off his horse, Aminet and the other wives were watching through a chink in the fence), not only was it impossible even to go to her, but it was impossible simply to lie down on his featherbed to rest from his weariness. It was necessary before all to perform the midday namaz, for which he now had not the slightest inclination, but which it was not only impossible for him not to fulfill in his position as religious leader of his people, but which for him was as necessary as daily food. And so he performed the ablution and the prayer. On finishing the prayer, he summoned those who were waiting for him.

The first to come in was his father-in-law and teacher, a tall, gray-haired, seemly-looking old man with a beard white as snow and a ruddy red face, Jemal ed-Din, who, after saying a prayer, began asking Shamil questions about the events of the campaign and telling him what had happened in the mountains during his absence.

Among all sorts of events—killings in blood feuds, thefts of cattle, accusations of the non-observance of the tariqat: smoking tobacco, drinking wine—Jemal ed-Din told him that Hadji Murat had sent men to take his family out to the Russians, but it had been discovered, and the family had been brought to Vedeno, where it was kept under watch, awaiting the imam's decision. The old men had gathered here in the kunak room to discuss all these matters, and Jemal ed-Din advised Shamil to allow it today, because they had already been waiting three days for him.

Having eaten dinner in his own room, brought to him by Zaidet, his sharp-nosed, dark, unpleasant-looking and unloved but eldest wife, Shamil went to the kunak room.

The six men who made up his council, old men with white, gray, or red beards, with or without turbans, in tall papakhas and new beshmets and cherkeskas, girded by belts with daggers, rose to meet him. Shamil was a head taller than all of them. They all lifted their hands palms up, as he did, and, closing their eyes, recited a prayer, then wiped their faces with their hands, bringing them down along their beards and joining them together. On finishing that, they all sat down, Shamil in the center on a higher pillow, and began the discussion of all the matters before them.

The cases of persons accused of crimes were decided according to the shariat: two men were sentenced to have a hand cut off for theft, another to have his head cut off for murder, and three were pardoned. Then they went on to the chief matter: considering the measures to be taken against Chechens going over to the Russians. To oppose these defections, Jemal ed-Din had drawn up the following proclamation:

"I wish you eternal peace with God Almighty. I hear that the Russians cajole you and call you to submission. Do not believe them and do not submit, but endure. If you are not rewarded for it in this life, you will be rewarded in the life to come. Remember what happened before, when your weapons were taken away. If God had not brought you to reason then, in 1840, you would now be soldiers and carry bayonets instead of daggers, and your wives would be going about without sharovary and would be dishonored. Judge the future by the past. It is better to die in enmity with the Russians than to live with infidels. Endure, and I will come to you with the Koran and the saber and lead you against the Russians. But now I strictly order you to have not only no intention, but even no thought of submitting to the Russians."

Shamil approved this proclamation and, having signed it, decided to have it sent out.

After these matters, the matter of Hadji Murat was also discussed. This matter was very important for Shamil. Though he did not want to admit it, he knew that if Hadji Murat, with his agility, boldness, and courage, had been with him, what had now happened in Chechnya would not have happened. To make peace with Hadji Murat and avail himself of his services again would be a good thing; if that was impossible, it was still impossible to allow him to aid the Russians. And therefore, in any case, it was necessary to make him come back and, once back, to kill him. The means for that was either to send a man to Tiflis who would kill him there, or to make him come here and here put an end to him. There was one means for doing that—his family, and above all his son, whom Shamil knew Hadji Murat loved passionately. And therefore it was necessary to act through the son.

When the councillors had discussed it, Shamil closed his eyes and fell silent.

The councillors knew that this meant he was now listening to the voice of the Prophet speaking to him, prescribing what should be done. After a solemn five-minute silence, Shamil opened his eyes, narrowed them more than usual, and said:

"Bring Hadji Murat's son to me."

"He's here," said Jemal ed-Din.

And indeed Yusuf, Hadji Murat's son, thin, pale, ragged, and stinking, but still handsome in face and body, with the same jet-black eyes as his grandmother Patimat, was already standing at the gate of the outer courtyard waiting to be summoned.

Yusuf did not share his father's feeling for Shamil. He did not know the whole past, or else he did, but, not having lived it, he did not understand why his father was so stubbornly hostile to Shamil. To him, who wanted only one thing—to go on with that easy, dissipated life he had led in Khunzakh as the naïb's son—it seemed totally unnecessary to be hostile to Shamil. In resistance and opposition to his father, he especially admired Shamil and felt the ecstatic veneration for him so widespread in the mountains. With a special feeling of trembling awe of the imam, he now entered the kunak room and, stopping in the doorway, met Shamil's intent, narrowed gaze. He stood there for some time, then went up to Shamil and kissed his big white hand with its long fingers.

"You are Hadji Murat's son?"

"Yes, imam."

"Do you know what he has done?"

"I do, imam, and I am sorry for it."

"Do you know how to write?"

"I was preparing to be a mullah."

"Then write to your father that if he comes back to me now, before bairam, I will forgive him and everything will be as before. If he does not and stays with the Russians, then"—Shamil frowned terribly—"I will hand your grandmother and your mother over to the aouls, and cut your head off."

Not a muscle twitched in Yusuf's face; he bowed his head as a sign that he had understood Shamil's words.

"Write that and give it to my messenger."

Shamil fell silent and looked at Yusuf for a long time.

"Write that I have had pity on you and will not kill you, but will put your eyes out, as I do with all traitors. Go."

Yusuf seemed calm in Shamil's presence, but once he was led out of the kunak room, he fell upon the man who was leading him and, snatching his dagger from its scabbard, tried to kill himself with it, but was seized by the arms, bound, and taken back to the hole.

THAT EVENING, when the evening prayers were over and dusk was falling, Shamil put on his white fur coat and went outside the fence to the part of the courtyard where his wives were quartered, and headed for Aminet's room. But Aminet was not there. She was with the older wives. Then Shamil, trying to go unnoticed, stood behind the door of the room, waiting for her. But Aminet was cross with Shamil, because he had given some silk not to her but to Zaidet. She saw how he came out and went to her room, looking for her, and purposely did not go there. She stood for a long time at the door of Zaidet's room and, laughing quietly, watched the white figure going in and out of her room. Having waited for her in vain, Shamil went back to his quarters when it was already time for the midnight prayers.

XX

HADJI MURAT HAD BEEN LIVING for a week in Ivan Matveevich's house in the fortress. Though Marya Dmitrievna quarreled with the shaggy Hanefi (Hadji Murat had taken only two men with him: Hanefi and Eldar) and chucked him out of the kitchen once, for which he nearly put a knife in her, she obviously had special feelings of respect and sympathy for Hadji Murat. She no longer served him dinner, having handed that task over to Eldar, but she profited from every chance to see him and please him. She also took the liveliest interest in the negotiations about his family, knew how many wives and children he had, how old they were, and each time a scout came, asked whomever she could about the results of the negotiations.

Butler became very friendly with Hadji Murat during that week.

Sometimes Hadji Murat came to his room, sometimes Butler went to him. Sometimes they conversed through an interpreter, sometimes by their own means—signs and, above all, smiles. Hadji Murat obviously came to love Butler. That was clear from Eldar's attitude toward Butler. When Butler came to Hadji Murat's room, Eldar met him, joyfully baring his gleaming teeth, and rushed to give him pillows to sit on and took off his saber, if he was wearing it.

Butler also made the acquaintance of and became close with shaggy Hanefi, Hadji Murat's sworn brother. Hanefi knew many mountaineer songs and sang them well. Hadji Murat, to please Butler, would send for Hanefi and order him to sing, naming the songs he considered good. Hanefi had a high tenor voice, and sang with extraordinary distinctness and expression. Hadji Murat especially liked one song, and Butler was struck by its solemn, sad melody. Butler asked the interpreter to tell over its content and wrote it down.

The song had to do with a blood feud—the very one that had existed between Hanefi and Hadji Murat.

It went like this:

"The earth will dry on my grave, and you will forget me, my mother! The graveyard will overgrow with the grass of the graves, and the grass will stifle your grief, my old father. The tears will dry in my sister's eyes, and the grief will fly from her heart.

"But you will not forget me, my older brother, as long as you have not avenged my death. And you will not forget me, my second brother, as long as you're not lying here beside me.

"Hot you are, bullet, and it's death you bear, but have you not been my faithful slave? Black, black earth, you will cover me, but did I not trample you with my horse? Cold you are, death, but I was your master. The earth will take my body, but heaven will receive my soul."

Hadji Murat always listened to this song with closed eyes, and when it ended on a drawn-out, dying-away note, always said in Russian:

"Good song, wise song."

The special, energetic poetry of the mountaineers' life caught Butler up still more with the arrival of Hadji Murat and his closeness with him and his murids. He acquired a beshmet, a cherkeska, leggings, and it seemed to him that he was himself a mountaineer and was living the same life as these people.

On the day of Hadji Murat's departure, Ivan Matveevich gathered several officers to see him off. Some of the officers were sitting at the tea table, where Marya Dmitrievna was serving tea, some at another table, with vodka, chikhir, and snacks, when Hadji Murat, dressed for the road and armed, stepping softly and quickly, came limping into the room.

They all stood up and shook hands with him one by one. Ivan Matveevich invited him to sit on the divan, but he thanked him and sat on a chair by the window. The silence that fell when he came in obviously did not embarrass him in the least. He looked around attentively at all the faces and rested his indifferent gaze on the table with the samovar and snacks. The sprightly officer Petrokovsky, who was seeing Hadji Murat for the first time, asked him through the interpreter whether he liked Tiflis.

"Aya," he said.

"He says 'Yes,' " replied the interpreter.

"What did he like?"

Hadji Murat said something in reply.

"He liked the theater most of all."

"Well, and did he like the ball at the commander in chief's?"

Hadji Murat frowned.

"Every people has its own customs. Our women do not dress that way," he said, glancing at Marya Dmitrievna.

"So he didn't like it?"

"We have a proverb," he said to the interpreter. "The dog treated the ass to meat, the ass treated the dog to hay—and both went hungry." He smiled. "Every people finds its own customs good."

The conversation went no further. Some of the officers began to take tea, some to eat. Hadji Murat took the offered glass of tea and placed it in front of him.

"What else? Cream? A roll?" said Marya Dmitrievna, offering them to him.

Hadji Murat inclined his head.

"Well, good-bye, then!" said Butler, touching his knee. "When will we see each other?"

"Good-bye! Good-bye!" Hadji Murat said in Russian, smiling. "*Kunak bulur.* You strong *kunak*. Time—*aida*—go," he said, tossing his head as if in the direction in which he had to go.

In the doorway of the room Eldar appeared with something big and white over his shoulder and a saber in his hand. Hadji Murat beckoned to him, and Eldar went over to Hadji Murat with his long strides and handed him the white burka and the saber. Hadji Murat stood up and took the burka and, throwing it over his arm, offered it to Marya Dmitrievna, saying something to the interpreter. The interpreter said:

"He says you praised the burka, so take it."

"What for?" said Marya Dmitrievna, blushing.

"It must be so. *Adat so*," said Hadji Murat.

"Well, thank you," said Marya Dmitrievna, taking the burka. "God grant you rescue your son. *Ulan yakshi*," she added. "Translate for him that I wish him the rescue of his family."

Hadji Murat glanced at Marya Dmitrievna and nodded his head approvingly. Then he took the saber from Eldar's hands and gave it to Ivan Matveevich. Ivan Matveevich took the saber and said to the interpreter:

"Tell him to take my brown gelding, I have nothing else to give him in return."

Hadji Murat waved his hand before his face, indicating that he needed nothing and would not take it, and then, pointing to the mountains and then to his heart, went to the door. They all followed after him. The officers who stayed inside drew the saber, examined its blade, and decided that it was a real Gurda.[19]

Butler went out to the porch along with Hadji Murat. But here something happened that no one expected and that might have ended with Hadji Murat's death, had it not been for his quick wits, resoluteness, and agility.

The inhabitants of the Kumyk aoul of Tash-Kichu, who had great respect for Hadji Murat and had come to the fortress many times just to look at the famous naïb, had sent envoys to Hadji Murat three days before his departure inviting him to their mosque on Friday. But the Kumyk princes, who lived in Tash-Kichu and hated Hadji Murat and had a blood feud with him, learned of it and announced to the people that they would not allow Hadji Murat into the mosque. The people became agitated, and a fight took place between them and the princes' adherents. The Russian authorities pacified the mountaineers and sent word to Hadji Murat that he should not come to the mosque. Hadji Murat did not go, and everyone thought the matter ended with that.

But at the very moment of Hadji Murat's departure, when he came out to the porch and the horses were standing ready, the Kumyk prince Arslan Khan, whom Butler and Ivan Matveevich knew, rode up to Ivan Matveevich's house.

Seeing Hadji Murat, he snatched a pistol from his belt and aimed it at him. But before Arslan Khan had time to fire, Hadji Murat, despite his lameness, like a cat, suddenly rushed at him from the porch. Arslan Khan fired and missed. Hadji Murat, running up to him, seized the bridle of his horse with one hand, snatched out his dagger with the other, and shouted something in Tartar.

Butler and Eldar simultaneously ran up to the enemies and seized them by the arms. Ivan Matveevich also came out at the sound of the shot.

"What's the meaning of this, Arslan, starting such nastiness at my house!" he said, having learned what it was about. "It's not good, brother. Have your way when it's far away, but don't start slaughtering people on my doorstep."

Arslan Khan, a small man with black mustaches, all pale and trembling, got off his horse, gave Hadji Murat a spiteful look, and went inside with Ivan Matveevich. Hadji Murat returned to the horses, breathing heavily and smiling.

"Why did he want to kill him?" Butler asked through the interpreter.

"He says such is our law," the interpreter transmitted the words of Hadji Murat. "Arslan has to take revenge on him for blood. That's why he wanted to kill him."

"Well, and what if he overtakes him on the way?" asked Butler.

Hadji Murat smiled.

"If he kills me, it means Allah wants it so. Well, good-bye," he said again in Russian and, taking his horse by the withers, he ran his eyes over all those who had come to see him off and his affectionate gaze met that of Marya Dmitrievna.

"Good-bye, dear leddy," he said, addressing her. "Thanking you."

"God grant, God grant you rescue your family," Marya Dmitrievna repeated.

He did not understand her words, but did understand her sympathy for him and nodded his head to her.

"See that you don't forget your kunak," said Butler.

"Tell him I am his faithful friend, I will never forget him," he replied through the interpreter and, despite his crooked leg, as soon as he touched the stirrup, he quickly and lightly swung his body up onto the high saddle and, straightening his saber, feeling with a habitual gesture for his pistol, acquiring that especially proud, martial look with which a mountaineer sits his horse, he rode away from Ivan Matveevich's house. Hanefi and Eldar also got on their horses and, amicably taking leave of the hosts and officers, went off at a trot after their murshid.

As always, talk sprang up about the departing one.

"Brave fellow!"

"He rushed like a wolf at Arslan Khan, his face was completely changed."

"And he'll play us for fools. Must be a great rogue," said Petrokovsky.

"God grant us more such Russian rogues," Marya Dmitrievna suddenly mixed in vexedly. "He lived a week with us; we saw nothing but good from him," she said. "Courteous, wise, just."

"How did you find all that out?"

"I just did."

"Fell for him, eh?" said Ivan Matveevich, coming in. "No denying it."

"Well, so I fell for him. What is it to you? Only why run him down, if he's a good man? He's a Tartar, but he's good."

"True, Marya Dmitrievna," said Butler. "Good girl for defending him."

XXI

THE LIFE of the inhabitants of the advance fortresses on the Chechen line went on as before. There were two alerts after that, when platoons ran out and Cossacks and militia went galloping, but both times the mountaineers could not be caught. They escaped, and once in Vozdvizhenskoe they killed a Cossack and made off with eight Cossack horses that were being watered. There were no raids since that last time when the aoul was laid waste. But a major expedition into Greater Chechnya was expected as a consequence of the appointment of a new commander of the left flank, Prince Baryatinsky.

Prince Baryatinsky, a friend of the heir to the throne, the former commander of the Kabardinsky regiment, now, as chief of the entire left flank, immediately upon his arrival in Grozny assembled a detachment to continue carrying out the directives of the sovereign, of which Chernyshov had written to Vorontsov. The detachment assembled in Vozdvizhenskoe set off from there to occupy a position in the direction of Kurinskoe. The troops made camp there and were cutting down the forest.

Young Vorontsov lived in a magnificent cloth tent, and his wife, Marya Vassilievna, would come to the camp and often spent the night. Baryatinsky's relations with Marya Vassilievna were no secret from anyone, and therefore the non-court officers and soldiers abused her crudely, because, owing to her presence in the camp, they were sent on night patrol. The mountaineers ordinarily brought up guns and sent cannonballs into the camp. For the most part these cannonballs missed, and therefore in ordinary times no measures were taken against this fire; but to keep the mountaineers from bringing up guns and frightening Marya Vassilievna, patrols were sent out. To go on patrol every night so that a lady would not be frightened was insulting and disgusting, and Marya Vassilievna was berated in indecent terms by the soldiers and the officers not received in high society.

Butler also came to this detachment on leave from his fortress, in order to meet his messmates from the Corps of Pages,[20] who were gathered there, and his regiment mates serving in the Kurinsky regiment and as adjutants and orderly officers at headquarters. At first his visit was very merry. He stayed in Poltoratsky's tent and found many acquaintances there who welcomed him joyfully. He also went to see Vorontsov, whom he knew slightly, because at some point he had served in the same regiment with him. Vorontsov received him very affably, introduced him to Prince Baryatinsky, and invited him to the farewell dinner he was giving for General Kozlovsky, who had been commander of the left flank before Baryatinsky.

The dinner was magnificent. Six tents had been brought and placed side by side. Along the entire length of them there was a covered table, set with dinnerware and bottles. Everything was reminiscent of the life of the guards in Petersburg. At two o'clock they sat down at table. At the middle of the table sat Kozlovsky on one side and Baryatinsky on the other. On either side of Kozlovsky sat the Vorontsovs: the husband to his right, the wife to his left. All down both sides of the table sat the officers of the Kabardinsky and Kurinsky regiments. Butler and Poltoratsky sat next to each other, both chatting away merrily and drinking with the officers next to them. When it came to the roast and the orderlies started pouring glasses of champagne, Poltoratsky, with genuine alarm and regret, said to Butler:

"Our 'like' is going to disgrace himself."

"How so?"

"He's got to make a speech. And how can he?"

"Yes, brother, it's not the same as scaling barricades under a hail of bullets. And with a lady beside him at that, and all these court gentlemen. Really, he's a pity to see," the officers said among themselves.

But now the solemn moment had come. Baryatinsky stood up and, raising his glass, addressed a short speech to Kozlovsky. When Baryatinsky finished, Kozlovsky stood up and in a rather firm voice began:

"By the supreme will of His Majesty I am leaving you, I am parting from you, gentlemen officers," he said. "But always consider me, like, with you . . . Gentlemen, you are familiar, like, with the truth: one man doesn't make an army. Therefore, all the rewards that I have, like, received for my service, all the great bounties, like, showered upon me by the sovereign emperor, like, all my position and, like, my good name—all, decidedly all, like . . ." (here his voice trembled) "I, like, owe only to you, only to you, my dear friends!" And his wrinkled face wrinkled still more. He sobbed and tears welled up in his eyes. "From the bottom of my heart, I offer you, like, my sincere, heartfelt gratitude . . ."

Kozlovsky could not speak any further and, rising, began to embrace the officers who came up to him. Everyone was moved. The princess covered her face with her handkerchief. Prince Semyon Mikhailovich, his mouth twisted, was blinking his eyes. Many of the officers also became tearful. Butler, who knew Kozlovsky very little, could not hold back his tears. He was extremely pleased with it all. Then toasts began for Baryatinsky, for Vorontsov, for the officers, for the soldiers, and the guests left the dinner drunk both with wine and with the martial raptures to which they were so especially inclined.

The weather was wonderful, sunny, still, the air fresh and invigorating. From all sides came the crackle of bonfires, the sounds of singing. It seemed as though everyone was celebrating something. Butler, in the most happy, tenderhearted state of mind, went to Poltoratsky. At

Poltoratsky's some officers had gathered, a card table had been set up, and an adjutant had started a bank of a hundred roubles. Butler twice left the tent clutching his purse in his trouser pocket, but he finally could not control himself and, despite the word he had given himself and his brothers not to gamble, he started to punt.

And before an hour had gone by, Butler, all red, in a sweat, smeared with chalk, sat, both elbows propped on the table, and wrote under the cards creased for corners or transports[21] the amounts of his bets. He had lost so much that he was afraid to count up what was scored against him. He knew without counting that, putting in all the salary he could draw in advance, plus the price of his horse, he still could not cover the debt he had run up to the unknown adjutant. He would have gone on playing, but the adjutant, with a stern face, laid down his cards with his clean, white hands and began to count up Butler's chalk-written column. Butler abashedly begged his pardon because he could not pay at once all that he had lost, and said that he would have it sent from home, and, as he said it, he noticed that they all felt sorry for him, and that all of them, even Poltoratsky, avoided his eyes. This was his last evening. He need only not to have gambled, but to have gone to Vorontsov's, where he had been invited, "and all would be well," he thought. And now it was not only not well, it was terrible.

Having taken leave of his comrades and acquaintances, he went home and, on arriving, immediately went to sleep and slept for eighteen hours straight, as one usually sleeps after losing. From the fact that he asked her for fifty kopecks to tip the Cossack who accompanied him, and from his sad looks and curt replies, Marya Dmitrievna understood that he had lost, and lit into Ivan Matveevich for letting him go.

The next day Butler woke up past eleven and, remembering his situation, wanted to sink back into the oblivion from which he had just emerged, but it was impossible. He had to take measures to pay the four hundred and seventy roubles he owed to the stranger. One of these measures consisted in writing a letter to his brother, confessing his sin and begging him to send him five hundred roubles for this last time, against the mill that still remained their common possession. Then he wrote to a stingy female relation of his, asking her to let him have the same five hundred roubles at any interest she liked. Then he went to Ivan Matveevich and, knowing that he, or rather Marya Dmitrievna, had money, asked him to loan him five hundred roubles.

"I would," said Ivan Matveevich, "I would at once, but Mashka won't let me. These women, devil knows, they're so stingy. But you've got to get out of it, you've got to, devil take it. What about that devil, the sutler?"

But there was no point even in trying to borrow from the sutler. So Butler's salvation could come only from his brother or from the stingy female relation.

XXII

HAVING FAILED to achieve his goal in Chechnya, Hadji Murat returned to Tiflis and went to Vorontsov every day and, when he was received, begged him to gather the captive mountaineers and exchange them for his family. He said again that without that his hands were tied and he could not serve the Russians as he would like to and destroy Shamil. Vorontsov vaguely promised to do what he could, but kept putting it off, saying that he would decide the matter when General Argutinsky came to Tiflis and he could discuss it with him. Then Hadji Murat started asking Vorontsov to allow him to go and live for a time in Nukha, a small town in Transcaucasia, where he supposed it would be easier for him to carry on negotiations about his family with Shamil and with people devoted to him. Besides that, in Nukha, a Muslim town, there was a mosque, where it would be much easier for him to observe the prayers dictated by Muslim law. Vorontsov wrote to Petersburg about it, and meanwhile nevertheless gave Hadji Murat permission to move to Nukha.

For Vorontsov, for the Petersburg authorities, as for the majority of Russian people who knew the story of Hadji Murat, this story represented either a fortunate turn in the Caucasian war or simply an interesting occurrence; but for Hadji Murat it was, especially in recent days, a terrible turn in his life. He had fled from the mountains partly to save himself, partly out of hatred for Shamil, and, difficult as that flight had been, he had achieved his goal, and at first rejoiced in his success and actually considered plans for attacking Shamil. But it turned out that bringing his family over, which he had thought would be easy to arrange, proved more difficult than he had thought. Shamil had seized his family and was holding them captive, promising to hand the women over to the aouls and to kill or blind his son. Now Hadji Murat was moving to Nukha with the intention of trying, through his adherents in Daghestan, to wrest his family from Shamil by cunning or by force. The last scout who visited him in Nukha told him that some Avars devoted to him were planning to steal his family and come over to the Russians with them, but that the people prepared to do that were too few, and that they did not dare to do it in the place of the family's confinement, in Vedeno, but would do it only in case the family was transferred from Vedeno to some other place. Then they promised to do it on the way. Hadji Murat told him to tell his friends that he promised three thousand roubles for the rescue of his family.

In Nukha Hadji Murat was given a small five-room house not far from the mosque and the khan's palace. In the same house lived the officers attached to him, and his interpreter and his nukers. Hadji Murat's life passed in waiting for and receiving scouts from the mountains and in the horseback rides he was allowed to take in the neighborhood of Nukha.

Returning from his ride on 8 April, Hadji Murat learned that in his absence an official had arrived from Tiflis. Despite all his desire to learn what the official had brought, Hadji Murat, before going to the room where a police commissioner and the official were waiting for him, went to his own room and recited the midday prayer. When he finished the prayer, he came out to the other room, which served him as a drawing room and a reception room. The official from Tiflis, the fat little state councillor Kirillov, conveyed to Hadji Murat the wish of Vorontsov that he come to Tiflis by the twelfth for a meeting with Argutinsky.

"*Yakshi,*" Hadji Murat said angrily.

He did not like the official Kirillov.

"Have you brought the money?"

"I have," said Kirillov.

"It is for two weeks now," said Hadji Murat, and he held up ten fingers and then four. "Give it to me."

"You'll get it at once," said the official, taking a purse from his traveling bag. "What does he need money for?" he said in Russian to the commissioner, supposing that Hadji Murat would not understand, but Hadji Murat understood and glanced angrily at Kirillov. Taking out the money, Kirillov, wishing to strike up a conversation so as to have something to convey to Prince Vorontsov on his return, asked him through the interpreter whether he was bored here. Hadji Murat gave a contemptuous sidelong glance at the fat little man in civilian dress and with no weapons and did not reply. The interpreter repeated the question.

"Tell him I do not want to talk to him. Let him give me the money."

And, having said that, Hadji Murat again sat down at the table, ready to count the money.

When Kirillov had taken out the gold pieces and divided them into seven stacks of ten pieces each (Hadji Murat received five gold pieces a day), he moved them towards Hadji Murat. Hadji Murat swept the gold pieces into the sleeve of his cherkeska, stood up, and quite unexpectedly slapped the state councillor on his bald pate and started out of the room. The state councillor jumped up and told the interpreter to tell Hadji Murat that he dare not do that, because he held the rank of a colonel. The commissioner confirmed the same. But Hadji Murat nodded his head in a sign that he knew it, and walked out of the room.

"What can you do with him?" said the commissioner. "He'll stick a dagger in you and that's that. You can't talk with these devils. I can see he's getting frantic."

As soon as dusk fell, two scouts came from the mountains, bound up to the eyes in their bashlyks. The commissioner led them inside to Hadji Murat. One of the scouts was a beefy, dark Tavlin, the other a thin old man. The news they brought did not gladden Hadji Murat. His friends who had undertaken to rescue his family now refused outright, fearing Shamil, who threatened the most frightful punishments for those who should help Hadji Murat. Having listened to the scouts' story, Hadji Murat rested his hands on his crossed legs and, lowering his head in its papakha, remained silent for a long time. Hadji Murat was thinking, and thinking decisively. He knew that he was now thinking for the last time, and that a decision was necessary. Hadji Murat raised his head and, picking up two gold pieces, gave one to each of the scouts and said:

"Go."

"What will the answer be?"

"The answer will be as God grants. Go."

The scouts rose and left, and Hadji Murat went on sitting on the carpet, his elbows propped on his knees. He sat like that for a long time, thinking.

"What to do? Trust Shamil and return to him?" thought Hadji Murat.

"He's a fox—he'll deceive me. Even if he doesn't deceive me, to submit to the red-headed deceiver is impossible. It is impossible because now, after I've been with the Russians, he will never trust me," thought Hadji Murat.

And he remembered a Tavlinian tale about a falcon who was caught, lived with people, and then returned to his mountains to his own kind. He returned, but in jesses, and on the jesses there were little bells. And the falcons did not accept him. "Fly away," they said, "to where they put silver bells on you. We have no bells or jesses." The falcon did not want to leave his native land and stayed. But the other falcons did not accept him and pecked him to death.

"And so they will peck me to death," thought Hadji Murat.

"Stay here? Subjugate the Caucasus for the Russian tsar, earn glory, rank, wealth?"

"It's possible," he thought, recalling his meetings with Vorontsov and the old prince's flattering words.

"But I must decide at once, otherwise he will destroy my family."

All night Hadji Murat lay awake and thought.

XXIII

By the middle of the night his decision was formed. He decided that he must flee to the mountains and break into Vedeno with his faithful Avars, and either die or rescue his family. Whether he would bring his family back to the Russians or flee with them to Khunzakh and fight Shamil—Hadji Murat did not decide. He knew only that right now he must flee from the Russians to the mountains. And he at once began to carry out his decision. He took his black quilted beshmet from under his pillow and went to his nukers' quarters. They lived across the hall. As soon as he went out to the hall, the door to which was open, he was enveloped in the dewy freshness of the moonlit night, and his ears were struck by the whistling and trilling of several nightingales at once from the garden adjoining the house.

Hadji Murat crossed the hall and opened the door of his nukers' room. There was no light in this room, only the young moon in its first quarter shone through the window. A table and two chairs stood to one side, and all four nukers lay on rugs and burkas on the floor. Hanefi slept outside with the horses. Gamzalo, hearing the creak of the door, sat up, turned to look at Hadji Murat, and, recognizing him, lay down again. Eldar, who lay next to him, jumped up and began putting on his beshmet, waiting for orders. Kurban and Khan Mahoma went on sleeping. Hadji Murat put his beshmet on the table, and something solid in the beshmet struck the boards of the table. It was the gold pieces sewn into it.

"Sew these in, too," said Hadji Murat, handing Eldar the gold pieces he had received that day.

Eldar took the gold pieces and, going to a brighter spot, drew the small knife from under his dagger, and at once began to unstitch the lining of the beshmet. Gamzalo raised himself and sat with his legs crossed.

"And you, Gamzalo, tell our brave lads to look over their rifles and pistols and prepare cartridges. We'll have a long ride tomorrow," said Hadji Murat.

"We've got powder, we've got bullets. Everything will be ready," said Gamzalo, and he growled something incomprehensible.

Gamzalo understood why Hadji Murat had ordered the guns loaded. From the very beginning, and more and more strongly as time went on, he had been wishing for one thing: to kill, to cut down as many Russian dogs as he could and flee to the mountains. And now he saw that Hadji Murat wanted the same thing, and he was content.

When Hadji Murat left, Gamzalo woke up his comrades, and all four spent the whole night examining their rifles, pistols, priming, flints, changing the bad ones, pouring fresh powder in the pans, plugging cartridge pockets with measured charges of powder and bullets wrapped in oiled rags, sharpening sabers and daggers and greasing the blades with tallow.

Before daybreak Hadji Murat went out to the hall again to fetch water for his ablutions. In the hall the pre-dawn trilling of the nightingales could be heard, still louder and more rapid than during the night. In the nukers' room could be heard the measured hiss and whistle of steel against stone as daggers were sharpened. Hadji Murat dipped some water from the tub and had already gone back to his door when he heard in the murids' room, besides the sound of sharpening, also the high, thin voice of Hanefi singing a song he knew. He stopped and began to listen.

The song told of how the dzhigit Hamzat and his brave lads stole a herd of white horses from the Russian side. How the Russian prince then overtook him beyond the Terek and surrounded him with his army big as a forest. Then it sang of how Hamzat slaughtered all the horses and hid with his brave lads behind the bloody mound of dead horses and fought as long as there were bullets in their guns and daggers at their belts and blood in their veins. But before he died, Hamzat saw birds in the sky and shouted to them: "You birds of the air, fly to our homes, tell our sisters and mothers and the white-skinned maidens that we all died for the ghazavat. Tell them that our bodies will not lie in graves, but ravenous wolves will rend them and gnaw our bones, and black ravens will peck out our eyes."

With these words the song ended, and to these last words, sung to a mournful tune, was joined the cheerful voice of the merry Khan Mahoma, who cried out at the very end of the song, "*La ilaha il Allah*"—and gave a piercing shriek. Then everything became still, and again only the trilling and whistling of the nightingales in the garden could be heard and from behind the door the measured hiss and occasional whistle of steel rapidly sliding over stone.

Hadji Murat was so deep in thought that he did not notice he had tipped the jug and water was spilling from it. He shook his head at himself and went into his room.

Having completed his morning ablutions, Hadji Murat looked over his weapons and sat on his bed. He had nothing more to do. In order to ride out, he had to ask permission from the police commissioner. But it was still dark outside and the commissioner was still asleep.

Hanefi's song reminded him of another song, one that his mother had made up. This song told about something that had actually happened—it had happened when Hadji Murat was just born, but his mother had told him about it.

The song went like this:

"Your Damascus dagger tore my white breast, yet I put it to my little sun, my boy, I washed him in my hot blood, and the wound healed without herbs and roots, I did not fear death, nor will my dzhigit boy."

The words of this song were addressed to Hadji Murat's father, and the meaning of it was that, when Hadji Murat was born, the khan's wife also gave birth to her next son, Umma Khan, and she summoned Hadji Murat's mother, who had nursed her elder son, Abununtsal, to come to her as a nurse. But Patimat did not want to leave this son and said she would not go. Hadji Murat's father became angry and ordered her to go. When she refused again, he struck her with a dagger and would have killed her, if she had not been taken away. So she did not give him up and nursed him, and made up a song about it.

Hadji Murat remembered that his mother, as she laid him to sleep beside her under a fur coat on the roof of the saklya, sang this song to him, and he asked her to show him the place on her side where the scar of the wound was left. He saw his mother before him as if alive—not wrinkled, gray-haired, and gap-toothed as he had left her now, but young, beautiful, and so strong that, when he was five years old and already heavy, she had carried him over the mountains to his grandfather in a basket on her back.

And he remembered, too, his grandfather, wrinkled, with a little gray beard, a silversmith, as he chased silver with his sinewy hands and made his grandson recite prayers. He remembered a spring at the foot of a hill where he used to go to fetch water with his mother, clinging to her sharovary. He remembered a skinny dog who used to lick his face, and especially the smell and taste of smoke and sour milk, when he followed his mother to the shed, where she milked the cow and baked the milk. He remembered how his mother shaved his head for the first time and how surprised he was to see his round, bluish little head in the gleaming copper basin that hung on the wall.

And, remembering himself as little, he also remembered his beloved son Yusuf, whose head he himself had shaved for the first time. Now this Yusuf was already a handsome young dzhigit. He remembered his son as he was the last time he saw him. That was the day he rode out of Tselmes. His son brought him his horse and asked permission to accompany him. He was dressed and armed, and held his own horse by the bridle. Yusuf's ruddy, handsome young face and his whole tall, slender figure (he was taller than his father) breathed the courage of youth and the joy of life. His broad shoulders, despite his age, his broad, youthful hips and long, slender body, his long, strong arms, and the strength, suppleness, agility of all his movements were a joy to see, and his father always admired his son.

"You'd better stay. You're alone in the house now. Take care of your mother and your grandmother," Hadji Murat said.

And Hadji Murat remembered the expression of bravado and pride with which Yusuf, blushing with pleasure, said that, as long as he lived, no one would harm his mother and grandmother. Yusuf mounted his horse all the same and rode with his father as far as the brook. At the brook he turned back, and since then Hadji Murat had not seen his wife, his mother, or his son.

And this was the son that Shamil wanted to blind! Of what would be done to his wife and mother he did not even want to think.

These thoughts so agitated Hadji Murat that he could not go on sitting there. He jumped up and, limping, went quickly to the door and, opening it, called Eldar. The sun had not yet risen, but it was quite light. The nightingales were still singing.

"Go and tell the commissioner that I want to go for a ride, and saddle the horses," he said.

XXIV

BUTLER'S ONLY CONSOLATION at that time was the poetry of military life, to which he gave himself not only on duty, but in private life as well. Dressed in Circassian costume, he went caracoling on horseback and twice lay in ambush with Bogdanovich, though they did not catch or kill anyone either time. This boldness and his friendship with the notoriously brave Bogdanovich seemed to Butler to be something pleasant and important. He had paid his debt by borrowing the money from a Jew at enormous interest—that is, he had only deferred and avoided the unresolved situation. He tried not to think about his situation and, besides the poetry of martial life, sought oblivion in wine. He drank more and more, and morally became weaker and weaker from day to day. He no longer played the handsome Joseph in relation to Marya Dmitrievna,[22] but, on the contrary, began courting her crudely, but, to his surprise, met with a decided rebuff, which shamed him greatly.

At the end of April, a detachment came to the fortress, destined by Baryatinsky for a new movement across the whole of Chechnya, which was considered impassable. There were two companies of the Kabardinsky regiment, and these companies, according to an established custom of the Caucasus, were received as guests by the companies stationed in Kurinskoe. The soldiers were dispersed among the barracks and were treated not only to a supper of kasha and beef, but also to vodka, and the officers were lodged with officers and, as was done, the local officers treated the newcomers.

The regalement ended with drinking and singing, and Ivan Matveevich, very drunk, no longer red but pale gray, sat astride a chair and, snatching out his saber, cut down his imaginary enemies, and cursed, then guffawed, then embraced people, then sang his favorite song: "Shamil rose up in years gone by, too-ra-lee, too-ra-lye, in years gone by."

Butler was there. He tried to see the poetry of martial life in it, but deep in his heart he felt sorry for Ivan Matveevich, but to stop him was in no way possible. And Butler, the drink having gone to his head, quietly left and went home.

A full moon shone upon the white houses and the stones of the road. It was so bright that every little stone, straw, and bit of dung could be seen on the road. Nearing the house, Butler met Marya Dmitrievna in a kerchief that covered her head and shoulders. After the rebuff Marya Dmitrievna had given him, Butler, slightly ashamed, had avoided meeting her. Now, with the moonlight and after the wine he had drunk, Butler was glad of this meeting and again wanted to be tender with her.

"Where are you going?" he asked.

"To see how my old man's doing," she replied amicably. She had rejected his courtship quite sincerely and decisively, but had found it unpleasant that he had shunned her all the time recently.

"Why go looking for him—he'll come."

"Will he?"

"If he doesn't, they'll bring him."

"Right, and that's not good," said Marya Dmitrievna. "So I shouldn't go?"

"No, you shouldn't. Better let's go home."

Marya Dmitrievna turned and walked back home beside Butler. The moon shone so brightly that their shadows, moving along the road, had a moving halo around the heads. Butler looked at this halo around his head and was getting ready to tell her that he still liked her just as much, but he did not know how to begin. She was waiting for what he would say. Thus, in silence, they had already come quite close to home when some horsemen came riding around the corner. It was an officer with an escort.

"Who is God sending us now?" Marya Dmitrievna said and stepped aside.

The moon shone behind the rider, so that Marya Dmitrievna recognized him only when he had come almost even with them. It was the officer Kamenev, who had served formerly with Ivan Matveevich, and therefore Marya Dmitrievna knew him.

"Pyotr Nikolaevich, is that you?" Marya Dmitrievna addressed him.

"Himself," said Kamenev. "Ah, Butler! Greetings! You're not asleep yet? Strolling with Marya Dmitrievna? Watch out, you'll get it from Ivan Matveevich. Where is he?"

"Just listen," said Marya Dmitrievna, pointing in the direction from which the sounds of a tulumbas and songs were coming. "They're carousing."

"What, your people?"

"No, there are some from Khasav Yurt, they're living it up."

"Ah, that's good. I'll still have time. I only need to see him for a minute."

"What, on business?" asked Butler.

"Minor business."

"Good or bad?"

"That depends! For us it's good, but for somebody else it's rather nasty." And Kamenev laughed.

Just then the walkers and Kamenev reached Ivan Matveevich's house.

"Chikhirev!" Kamenev called to a Cossack. "Come here."

A Don Cossack moved away from the others and rode up to them. He was wearing an ordinary Don Cossack uniform, boots, a greatcoat, and had saddlebags behind his saddle.

"Well, take the thing out," said Kamenev, getting off his horse.

The Cossack also got off his horse and took a sack with something in it from his saddlebag. Kamenev took the sack from the Cossack's hands and put his hand into it.

"So, shall I show you our news? You won't be frightened?" he turned to Marya Dmitrievna.

"What's there to be afraid of?" said Marya Dmitrievna.

"Here it is," said Kamenev, taking out a human head and holding it up in the moonlight. "Recognize him?"

It was a head, shaved, with large projections of the skull over the eyes and a trimmed black beard and clipped mustache, with one eye open and the other half closed, the shaved skull split but not all the way through, the bloody nose clotted with black blood. The neck was wrapped in a bloody towel. Despite all the wounds to the head, the blue lips were formed into a kindly, childlike expression.

Marya Dmitrievna looked and, without saying a word, turned and went quickly into the house.

Butler could not take his eyes from the terrible head. It was the head of the same Hadji Murat with whom he had so recently spent evenings in such friendly conversation.

"How can it be? Who killed him? Where?" he asked.

"He tried to bolt and got caught," said Kamenev, and he handed the head back to the Cossack and went into the house with Butler.

"And he died a brave man," said Kamenev.

"But how did it all happen?"

"Just wait a little. Ivan Matveevich will come, and I'll tell you all about it in detail. That's why I've been sent. I carry it around to all the fortresses and aouls and display it."

They sent for Ivan Matveevich, and he came home drunk, with two officers just as badly drunk, and started embracing Kamenev.

"I've come to see you," said Kamenev. "I've brought the head of Hadji Murat."

"You're joking! Killed?"

"Yes, he tried to escape."

"I told you he'd play us for fools. So where is it? This head? Show me."

They called for the Cossack, and he brought in the sack with the head. The head was taken out, and Ivan Matveevich looked at it for a long time with drunken eyes.

"He was a fine fellow all the same," he said. "Let me kiss him."

"Yes, true, he was quite a daredevil," said one of the officers.

When they had all examined the head, it was handed back to the Cossack. The Cossack put the head into the sack, trying to lower it to the floor so that it would not bump too hard.

"And you, Kamenev, what do you tell people when you show it?" asked one of the officers.

"No, let me kiss him. He gave me a saber," cried Ivan Matveevich.

Butler went out to the porch. Marya Dmitrievna was sitting on the second step. She glanced at Butler and at once turned away angrily.

"What's the matter, Marya Dmitrievna?" asked Butler.

"You're all butchers. I can't bear it. Real butchers," she said, getting up.

"The same could happen to anyone," said Butler, not knowing what to say. "That's war."

"War!" cried Marya Dmitrievna. "What war? You're butchers, that's all. A dead body should be put in the ground, and they just jeer. Real butchers," she repeated and stepped off the porch and went into the house through the back door.

Butler went back to the drawing room and asked Kamenev to tell in detail how the whole thing happened.

And Kamenev told them.

It happened like this.

XXV

HADJI MURAT WAS ALLOWED to go riding in the vicinity of town, but only with a Cossack escort. There were some fifty Cossacks in Nukha, of whom some ten were attached to the superior officers, while the rest, if they were to be sent out ten at a time, as had been ordered, had to be detailed every other day. And therefore on the first day they sent ten Cossacks, and then decided to send five, asking Hadji Murat not to take all his nukers with him, but on 25 April Hadji Murat went out riding with all five of them. As Hadji Murat was mounting his horse, the commander noticed that all five nukers were about to go with him, and told him that he was not allowed to take them all, but Hadji Murat seemed not to hear, touched up his horse, and the commander did not insist. With the Cossacks there was a corporal with a bowl haircut, holder of a St. George's Cross, a young, ruddy, healthy, brown-haired lad named Nazarov. He was the eldest son of a poor family of Old Believers,[23] had grown up without a father, and supported his old mother, three sisters, and two brothers.

"Watch out, Nazarov, don't let them go too far!" cried the commander.

"Yes, sir, Your Honor," replied Nazarov and, rising in his stirrups and grasping the rifle at his back, he sent his good, big, hook-nosed sorrel gelding into a trot. Four Cossacks rode after him: Ferapontov, tall, skinny, a first-rate thief and double-dealer—the one who had sold powder to Gamzalo; Ignatov, serving out his term, no longer young, a robust peasant proud of his strength; Mishkin, a weakly youngster whom everyone made fun of; and Petrakov, young, fair-haired, his mother's only son, always cheerful and affectionate.

There was mist in the morning, but by breakfast time the weather cleared, and the sun glistened on the just-opening leaves, and on the young, virginal grass, and on the sprouting grain, and on the ripples of the swift river, which could be glimpsed to the left of the road.

Hadji Murat rode at a walk. The Cossacks and his nukers followed him without dropping back. They rode at a walk down the road outside the fortress. They met women with baskets on their heads, soldiers on wagons, and creaking carts drawn by buffaloes. After riding for about a mile and a half, Hadji Murat touched up his white Kabarda stallion; it went into a canter, so that his nukers had to switch to a long trot. The Cossacks did the same.

"Eh, he's got a good horse under him," said Ferapontov. "If only we weren't at peace, I'd unseat him."

"Yes, brother, three hundred roubles were offered for that horse in Tiflis."

"But I'll outrace him on mine," said Nazarov.

"Outrace him, ha!" said Ferapontov.

Hadji Murat kept increasing his pace.

"Hey, kunak, that's not allowed. Slow down!" cried Nazarov, going after Hadji Murat.

Hadji Murat looked back and, saying nothing, went on riding without diminishing his pace.

"Watch out, they're up to something, the devils," said Ignatov. "Look at 'em whipping along!"

They rode like that for about half a mile in the direction of the mountains.

"I said it's not allowed," Nazarov cried again.

Hadji Murat did not reply and did not look back, but only increased his pace and from a canter went into a gallop.

"Oh, no, you won't get away!" cried Nazarov, stung to the quick.

He whipped up his big sorrel gelding and, rising in the stirrups and leaning forward, sent him at full speed after Hadji Murat.

The sky was so clear, the air so fresh, the forces of life played so joyfully in Nazarov's soul as he merged into one with his good, strong horse and flew along the level road after Hadji Murat, that the possibility of anything bad or sad or terrible never entered his head. He rejoiced that with every stride he was gaining on Hadji Murat and coming closer to him. Hadji Murat figured from the hoofbeats of the Cossack's big horse, coming ever closer to him, that he would shortly overtake him, and, putting his right hand to his pistol, with his left he began to rein in his excited Kabarda, who could hear the hoofbeats of a horse behind him.

"It's not allowed, I said!" cried Nazarov, coming almost even with Hadji Murat and reaching out his hand to seize the horse's bridle. But before he could seize it, a shot rang out.

"What are you doing?" Nazarov cried, clutching his chest. "Strike them down, lads," he said and, reeling, fell onto his saddlebow.

But the mountaineers seized their weapons before the Cossacks and shot them with their pistols and slashed them with their sabers. Nazarov was hanging on the neck of his frightened horse, which carried him in circles around his comrades. Ignatov's horse fell under him, crushing his leg. Two of the mountaineers, drawing their sabers without dismounting, slashed at his head and arms. Petrakov made a dash for his comrade, but at once two shots, one in the back, the other in the side, seared him, and he tumbled from his horse like a sack.

Mishkin wheeled his horse around and galloped off to the fortress. Hanefi and Khan Mahoma rushed after Mishkin, but he was already far away and the mountaineers could not catch him.

Seeing that they could not catch the Cossack, Hanefi and Khan Mahoma went back to their own people. Gamzalo, having finished off Ignatov with his dagger, also put it into Nazarov, after pulling him from his horse. Khan Mahoma was taking pouches of shot from the dead men. Hanefi wanted to take Nazarov's horse, but Hadji Murat shouted that he should not and set off down the road. His murids galloped after him, driving away Petrakov's horse, who came running after them. They were already two miles from Nukha, in the midst of the rice fields, when a shot rang out from the tower sounding the alarm.

Petrakov lay on his back with his stomach slit open, and his young face was turned to the sky, and he blubbered like a fish as he was dying.

"O LORD, saints alive, what have they done!" cried the commander of the fortress, clutching his head, when he heard about Hadji Murat's escape. "My head will roll! They let him slip, the brigands!" he cried, hearing Mishkin's report.

The alarm was given everywhere, and not only were all the available Cossacks sent after the fugitives, but they gathered all the militia that could be gathered from the peaceful aouls. A thousand-rouble reward was offered to the one who would bring in Hadji Murat dead or alive. And two hours after Hadji Murat and his comrades galloped away from the Cossacks, more than two hundred mounted men galloped after the police commissioner to seek out and capture the fugitives.

Having ridden several miles along the high road, Hadji Murat reined in his heavily breathing white horse, who had gone gray with sweat, and stopped. To the right of the road the saklyas and minaret of the aoul of Belardzhik could be seen, to the left were fields, and at the end of them a river was visible. Though the way to the mountains was to the right, Hadji Murat turned in the opposite direction, to the left, reckoning that the pursuit would rush after him precisely to the right. Whereas he, leaving the road and crossing the Alazan, would come out on the high road, where no one would expect him, and would go down it to the forest, and then, crossing the river again, would make his way through the forest to the mountains. Having decided that, he turned to the left. But it proved impossible to reach the river. The rice field they had to ride through, as was always done in the spring, had just been flooded with water and had turned into a bog, into which the horses sank over their pasterns. Hadji Murat and his nukers turned right, left, thinking to find a drier place, but the field they had happened upon was all evenly flooded and now soaked with water. With the sound of corks popping, the horses pulled their sinking feet from the oozy mud and stopped after every few steps, breathing heavily.

They struggled like that for so long that dusk began to fall, but they still had not reached the river. To the left there was a little island of bushes coming into leaf, and Hadji Murat decided to ride into these bushes and stay there till night, giving a rest to the exhausted horses.

Having entered the bushes, Hadji Murat and his nukers dismounted and, after hobbling the horses, left them to feed, and themselves ate some bread and cheese that they had taken with them. The young moon, which shone at first, went down behind the mountains, and the night was dark. In Nukha there were especially many nightingales. There were two in these bushes. While Hadji Murat and his men made noise, entering the bushes, the nightingales fell silent. But when the men became quiet, they again began to trill and call to each other. Hadji Murat, his ear alert to the sounds of the night, involuntarily listened to them.

And their whistling reminded him of that song about Hamzat, which he had listened to the night before when he went out for water. At any moment now he could be in the same situation as Hamzat. It occurred to him that it even would be so, and his soul suddenly became serious. He spread out his burka and performed his namaz. He had only just finished when he heard sounds approaching the bushes. These were the sounds of a large number of horses' feet splashing through the bog. The quick-eyed Khan Mahoma, having run out alone to the edge of the bushes, spotted in the darkness the black shadows of men on horseback and on foot approaching the bushes. Hanefi saw a similar crowd on the other side. It was Karganov,[24] the district military commander, with his militia.

"So we shall fight like Hamzat," thought Hadji Murat.

After the alarm was given, Karganov, with a company of militia and Cossacks, had rushed in pursuit of Hadji Murat, but had not found him or any trace of him anywhere. Karganov was already returning home without hope when, towards evening, he met an old Tartar. Karganov asked the old man if he had seen six horsemen. The old man answered that he had. He had seen six horsemen circle about in the rice field and enter the bushes where he used to gather firewood. Karganov, taking the old man along, turned back and, convinced at the sight of the hobbled horses that Hadji Murat was there, surrounded the bushes during the night and waited for morning to take Hadji Murat dead or alive.

Realizing that he was surrounded, Hadji Murat spotted an old ditch among the bushes and decided to position himself in it and fight for as long as he had shot and strength. He said this to his comrades and told them to make a mound along the ditch. And the nukers set to work at once cutting branches and digging up the earth with their daggers, making an embankment. Hadji Murat worked with them.

As soon as it became light, the company commander rode up close to the bushes and called out:

"Hey! Hadji Murat! Surrender! There are many of us and few of you!"

In reply to that a puff of smoke appeared from the ditch, a rifle cracked, and a bullet struck the militiaman's horse, who shied under him and began to fall. Following that came a crackle of rifle fire from the militiamen standing at the edge of the bushes, and their bullets, whistling and droning, knocked off leaves and branches and struck the mound, but did not hit the people sitting behind it. Only Gamzalo's horse, who had strayed, was hurt by them. He was wounded in the head. He did not fall, but snapped his hobble and, crashing through the bushes, rushed to the other horses and, pressing himself against them, drenched the young grass with blood. Hadji Murat and his men fired only when one of the militiamen stepped out, and they rarely missed their aim. Three of the militiamen were wounded, and the militiamen not only did not venture to rush Hadji Murat and his men, but retreated further and further from them and fired only from a distance, at random.

It went on like that for more than an hour. The sun had risen half the height of a tree, and Hadji Murat was already thinking of mounting up and trying to get through to the river, when he heard the shouts of a large party that had just arrived. This was Ghadji Aga of Mekhtuli with his men. There were about two hundred of them. Ghadji Aga had once been Hadji Murat's kunak and had lived with him in the mountains, but then had gone over to the Russians. With him was Akhmet Khan, the son
of Hadji Murat's enemy. Ghadji Aga, like Karganov, began by shouting to Hadji Murat to surrender, but, like the first time, Hadji Murat replied with a shot.

"Sabers out, lads!" cried Ghadji Aga, snatching out his own, and a hundred voices were heard as men rushed shrieking into the bushes.

The militiamen ran into the bushes, but from behind the mound several shots cracked out one after the other. Three men fell, and the attackers stopped and also started firing from the edge of the bushes. They fired and at the same time gradually approached the mound, running from bush to bush. Some managed to make it, some fell under the bullets of Hadji Murat and his men. Hadji Murat never missed, and Gamzalo also rarely wasted a shot and shrieked joyfully each time he saw his bullet hit home. Kurban was sitting on the edge of the ditch, singing *"La ilaha il Allah"* and firing unhurriedly, but rarely hitting anything. Eldar was trembling all over from impatience to rush at the enemies with his dagger and fired frequently and at random, constantly turning to look at Hadji Murat and thrusting himself up from behind the mound. The shaggy Hanefi, his sleeves rolled up, performed the duties of a servant here, too. He loaded the guns that Hadji Murat and Kurban passed to him, taking bullets wrapped in oiled rags and carefully ramming them home with an iron ramrod, and pouring dry powder into the pans from a flask. Khan Mahoma did not sit in the ditch like the others, but kept running between the ditch and the horses, driving them to a safer place, and constantly shrieked and fired freehand without a prop. He was the first to be wounded. A bullet hit him in the neck, and he sat down, spitting blood and cursing. Then Hadji Murat was wounded. A bullet pierced his shoulder. Hadji Murat pulled some cotton wool from his beshmet, stopped the wound with it, and went on firing.

"Let's rush them with our sabers," Eldar said for the third time.

He thrust himself up from behind the mound, ready to rush at his enemies, but just then a bullet hit him, and he reeled and fell backwards onto Hadji Murat's leg. Hadji Murat glanced at him. The beautiful sheep's eyes looked at Hadji Murat intently and gravely. The mouth, its upper lip pouting like a child's, twitched without opening. Hadji Murat freed his leg from under him and went on aiming. Hanefi bent over the slain Eldar and quickly began taking the unused cartridges from his cherkeska. Kurban, singing all the while, slowly loaded and took aim.

The enemy, running from bush to bush with whoops and shrieks, was moving closer and closer. Another bullet hit Hadji Murat in the left side. He lay back in the ditch and, tearing another wad of cotton wool from his beshmet, stopped the wound. This wound in the side was fatal, and he felt that he was dying. Memories and images replaced one another with extraordinary swiftness in his imagination. Now he saw before him the mighty Abununtsal Khan, holding in place his severed, hanging cheek as he rushed at the enemy with a dagger in his hand; now he saw the weak, bloodless old Vorontsov, with his sly, white face, and heard his soft voice; now he saw his son Yusuf, now his wife Sofiat, now the pale face, red beard, and narrowed eyes of his enemy Shamil.

And all these memories ran through his imagination without calling up any feeling in him: no pity, no anger, no desire of any sort. It all seemed so insignificant compared with what was beginning and had already begun for him. But meanwhile his strong body went on doing what had been started. He gathered his last strength, rose up from behind the mound, and fired his pistol at a man running towards him and hit him. The man fell. Then he got out of the hole altogether and, limping badly, walked straight ahead with his dagger to meet his enemies. Several shots rang out, he staggered and fell. Several militiamen, with a triumphant shriek, rushed to the fallen body. But what had seemed to them a dead body suddenly stirred. First the bloodied, shaven head, without a papakha, rose, then the body rose, and then, catching hold of a tree, he rose up entirely. He looked so terrible that the men running at him stopped. But he suddenly shuddered, staggered away from the tree, and, like a mowed-down thistle, fell full length on his face and no longer moved.

He no longer moved, but he still felt. When Ghadji Aga, who was the first to run up to him, struck him on the head with his big dagger, it seemed to him that he had been hit with a hammer, and he could not understand who was doing it and why. That was his last conscious connection with his body. After that he no longer felt anything, and his enemies trampled and hacked at what no longer had anything in common with him. Ghadji Aga, placing his foot on the back of the body, cut the head off with two strokes, and carefully, so as not to stain his chuviaki with blood, rolled it aside with his foot. Bright red blood gushed from the neck arteries and black blood from the head, flowing over the grass.

Karganov, and Ghadji Aga, and Akhmet Khan, and all the militiamen, like hunters over a slain animal, gathered over the bodies of Hadji Murat and his men (Hanefi, Kurban, and Gamzalo had been bound) and, standing there in the bushes amid the powder smoke, talked merrily, exulting in their victory.

The nightingales, who had fallen silent during the shooting, again started trilling, first one close by and then others further off.

THIS WAS the death I was reminded of by the crushed thistle in the midst of the plowed field.

1896–1904

GLOSSARY OF CAUCASIAN MOUNTAINEER WORDS

(The speech of the Caucasus is made up of words from Tartar, Persian, Arabic, Chechen, Nogai, and other local languages. Accents have been added to indicate pronunciation.)

ADÁT Custom
AIDÁ Come
AMANÁT Hostage
AÓUL Tartar mountain village
AYA Yes
BAIRÁM Name of two Muslim festivals: Uraza (Lesser) Bairam, which ends the fast of Ramadan, and Kurban (Greater) Bairam, which comes seventy days later and commemorates the story of Abraham and Isaac
BAR Have
BASHLÝK Hood with long ends wrapped around the neck as a scarf
BESHMÉT Upper garment fitted and buttoned from waist to neck and hanging to the knees
BÚRKA Long, round felt cape with decorative fastening at the neck
CHERKÉSKA Outer garment overlapping on the chest and belted, with rows of individual cartridge pockets on each side, worn over the beshmet
CHIKHÍR Young red wine
CHINÁRA Plane tree
CHUVIÁKI Soft leather shoes, often worn under wooden shoes
DZHIGÍT Bold, showy horseman, fine fellow, "brave"
GIAÓUR Perjorative term applied by Muslims to non-Muslims, especially Christians
GHAZAVÁT Muslim holy war against infidels

IMÁM Muslim priest, leader or chief combining worldly and spiritual authority

KHAN Originally a title given to the successors of Genghis Khan; later a common title given even to very minor rulers or officials in Central Asia; Russians created the word *khansha* for a khan's wife

KIZYÁK Fuel made from dung and straw

KOSHKÓLDY Good health and peace (greeting)

KUMGÁN Tall jar with spout and lid

KUNÁK Sworn friend, adoptive brother

MURÍD One who follows the mystical-religious path of Muridis, a movement that spread through the northern Caucasus in the nineteenth century, a form of Sufism connected with aspiration for an Islamic state free of Russian dominance; used here to mean adjutant or bodyguard

MURSHÍD One who leads murids on the path

NAÏB Lieutenant or administrator appointed by the imam Shamil

NAMÁZ Muslim prayers and ablutions performed five times a day

NOGÁI A Tartar people said to be descended from Nogai Khan, grandson of Genghis Khan, settled in Daghestan, Cherkessia, and along the Black Sea

NÚKER Attendant, bodyguard

PAPÁKHA Tall hat, usually of lambskin, often with a flat top

PESHKÉSH Gift

SÁKLYA Clay-plastered house, often built of earth, with a large shaded porch in front

SALÁAM ALÉIKUM Peace be with you (greeting)

SARDÁR Chief administrator or military commander; title given to the Russian emperor's representative in the Caucasus

SAUBÚL Good health to you (greeting)

SHARIÁT Islamic written law, in the Koran and other texts

SHAROVÁRY Balloon trousers

TARIQÁT The "path" (rules) of ascetic life

TULÚMBAS A percussion instrument

YAKSHÍ Good

YOK No, not

NOTES

1. Shamil (1797–1871) was the third imam (military-religious leader) of Daghestan and Chechnya to lead his people against the Russians, who sought to annex their land. He finally surrendered in 1859.

2. Prince Semyon Mikhailovich Vorontsov (1823–82) was an imperial adjutant and commander of the Kurinsky regiment. His early service was under his father, who was vicegerent of the Caucasus. He was married to Princess Marya Vassilievna Trubetskoy.

3. Vladimir Alexeevich Poltoratsky (1828–89) began his service in the Caucasus and rose to the rank of general. Tolstoy used material from his memoirs in writing *Hadji Murat.*

4. The Avars were a nomadic proto-Turkish people of the Hun family from so-called Tartary, a vast territory in Central Asia stretching from the Urals to the Pacific. By the nineteenth century, their remnant occupied part of Circassia and was ruled by its own khan. Hadji Murat was an Avar, as was the imam Shamil. Later Hanefi is referred to as a Tavlin, which is another name for Avar.

5. The phrase *La ilaha il Allah* ("There is no god but Allah"), which states the most central belief of Islam, is sung in the call to prayer five times a day and may also be used as a battle cry.

6. Abraham Louis Breguet (1747–1823), the most famous of Swiss watchmakers, founded a factory in Paris in 1775. A great innovator, he invented the self-winding watch and the "repeater," which rings the hours.

7. See note 4 to *Master and Man.*

8. Mikhail Semyonovich Vorontsov (1782–1856) was a field marshal during the Napoleonic wars. Later he was made governor general of the new southern provinces of Russia, with their capital in Odessa. In 1844 he was named vicegerent of the Caucasus and awarded the title of prince. Between 1844 and 1853, he led a number of expeditions into the Caucasian mountains. In 1853 he retired to Odessa.

9. In fact, at the battle of Craonne, between Reims and Soissons on the north bank of the Aisne, on 7 March 1814, Napoleon led a force of 37,000 men against an army of 85,000 Russians and Prussians under the command of General Blücher and gained a clear victory, though with heavy losses.

10. Joachim Murat (1767–1815) was a cavalry commander and one of Napoleon's most important generals. He married the emperor's sister Caroline in 1800.

11. Franz Karlovich Klugenau (1791–1851), a lieutenant general, was commander of the Russian army of northern Daghestan. Tolstoy made use of his correspondence with Hadji Murat and of his journals.

12. Mikhail Tarielovich Loris-Melikov (1825–88) later became an important statesman and finally minister of the interior. In chapters XI and XIII, Tolstoy used Loris-Melikov's actual transcript of his conversations with Hadji Murat.

13. Kazi Mullah (1794–1832) was the first imam of Daghestan and Chechnya to take up the ghazavat (holy war) against the Russians. He was killed in battle and was replaced as imam by Hamzat Bek (1797–1834).

14. In 1785, Sheikh Mansur (Elisha Mansur Ushurma, 1732–94), taking the title, not of imam, but of "preparatory mover," preached unity among the Caucasian Muslims in a holy war against the Russians. In 1791 his forces were defeated by Prince Potemkin at Anapa, and Mansur was captured and taken to Petersburg, where he was imprisoned for life.

15. Tolstoy gives his own translation of Vorontsov's actual letter. Alexander Ivanovich Chernyshov (1785–1857) was a Russian cavalry commander and adjutant general during the Napoleonic wars. He served as minister of war from 1827 to 1852 and was chairman of the State Council.

16. Count Zakhar Grigorievich Chernyshov (1797–1862), no relation to the minister of war, was a Decembrist and member of the Northern Secret Society of young noblemen whose aim was to make Russia a constitutional monarchy, if not a republic. His namesake, then General A. I. Chernyshov, was instrumental in crushing the Decembrist uprising of 1825, in which Zakhar Grigorievich took no actual part, but for which he was tried and sentenced along with other members of the Northern Society. The general did indeed try to take his inheritance.

17. The Eastern Catholic Church, Catholic Church of the Eastern Rite, or Uniate Church, existing in the Ukraine and western Russia, accepts the authority of the See of Rome, but follows Eastern Orthodox liturgical practices. The Great Schism between the Roman Catholic and Eastern Orthodox Churches occurred in 1054.

18. A prayer for health, prosperity, and "many years" of life for the person concerned is recited and sung at the end of the liturgy or on other occasions.

19. In a note to his novel *The Cossacks* (1862), Tolstoy wrote: "The most valued sabers and daggers in the Caucasus are called Gurda, after their maker."

20. The imperial Corps of Pages was an elite military school founded in 1697 by Peter the Great for training aristocratic boys in personal attendance on the emperor. Graduates had the unique privilege of joining any regiment they chose, regardless of openings.

21. "Corners" and "transports" are terms from the game of shtoss, a gambling game similar to basset or the American faro, very popular in the eighteenth and nineteenth centuries.

22. In the biblical story of Joseph (Genesis 37–50), the young and handsome Joseph treats his master's wife with the utmost respect and prudence.

23. The Old Believers, also known as Raskolniki (schismatics), rejected the reforms introduced in the mid-seventeenth century by the patriarch Nikon (1605-81), head of the Russian Orthodox Church. Historically, their relations with the civil administration were often strained.

24. Iosif Ivanovich Karganov was the military commander of Nukha. Hadji Murat lived in his house before his flight. Tolstoy was in touch with Karganov's widow, who supplied him with details about Hadji Murat's knowledge of Russian, his horses, his lameness, the appearance of his murids, and about his flight and death.

ALSO TRANSLATED BY RICHARD PEVEAR AND LARISSA VOLOKHONSKY

BY LEO TOLSTOY

THE DEATH OF IVAN ILYICH

Tolstoy's most famous novella is an intense and moving examination of death and the possibilities of redemption, here in a powerful translation by the award-winning Richard Pevear and Larissa Volokhonsky. Ivan Ilyich is a middle-aged man who has spent his life focused on his career as a bureaucrat and emotionally detached from his wife and children. After an accident he finds himself on the brink of an untimely death, which he sees as a terrible injustice. Face to face with his mortality, Ivan begins to question everything he has believed about the meaning of life. *The Death of Ivan Ilyich* is a masterpiece of psychological realism and philosophical profundity that has inspired generations of readers.

Fiction/Literature

WAR AND PEACE

War and Peace broadly focuses on Napoleon's invasion of Russia in 1812 and follows three of the most well-known characters in literature: Pierre Bezukhov, the illegitimate son of a count who is fighting for his inheritance and yearning for spiritual fulfillment; Prince Andrei Bolkonsky, who leaves his family behind to fight in the war against Napoleon; and Natasha Rostov, the beautiful young daughter of a nobleman who intrigues both men. As Napoleon's army invades, Tolstoy brilliantly follows characters from diverse backgrounds—peasants and nobility, civilians and soldiers—as they struggle with the problems unique to their era, their history, and their culture. And as the novel progresses, these characters transcend their specificity, becoming some of the most moving—and human—figures in world literature.

Fiction/Literature

BY FYODOR DOSTOEVSKY

THE ADOLESCENT

The protagonist of *The Adolescent* is Arkady Dolgoruky, a naïve nineteen-year-old boy bursting with ambition and opinions. The illegitimate son of a dissipated landowner, he is torn between his desire to expose his father's wrongdoing and the desire to win his love. He travels to St. Petersburg to confront the father he barely knows, inspired by an inchoate dream of communion and armed with a document that he believes gives him power over others. This new English version by the most acclaimed of Dostoevsky's translators is a masterpiece of pathos and high comedy.

Fiction/Literature

CRIME AND PUNISHMENT

It is a murder story, told from the murderer's point of view, that implicates even the most innocent reader in its enormities. It is a cat-and-mouse game between a tormented young killer and a cheerfully implacable detective. It is a preternaturally acute investigation of the forces that impel a man toward sin, suffering, and grace. Richard Pevear and Larissa Volokhonsky have rendered this elusive and inventive novel with an energy, suppleness, and range of voice that do full justice to the genius of its creator.

Fiction/Literature

DEMONS

Inspired by a political murder that horrified Russians in 1869, Dostoevsky conceived *Demons* as a "novel-pamphlet" in which he articulated the plague of materialist ideology that he saw infecting his native land. What emerged was his darkest novel until *The Brothers Karamazov* and his most ferociously funny. For alongside its relentlessly escalating plot of conspiracy and assassination, *Demons* is a blistering comedy of ideas run amok.

Fiction/Literature

THE IDIOT

The twenty-six-year-old Prince Myshkin, following a stay of several years in a Swiss sanatorium, returns to Russia to collect an inheritance and "be among people." Even before he reaches home he meets the dark Rogozhin, a rich merchant's son whose obsession with the beautiful Nastasya Filippovna eventually draws all three of them into a tragic denouement. In Petersburg the prince finds himself a stranger in a society obsessed with money, power, and manipulation. Scandal escalates to murder as Dostoevsky traces the surprising effect of this "positively beautiful man" on the people around him.

Fiction/Literature

NOTES FROM UNDERGROUND

"I am a sick man . . . I am a wicked man." With this sentence Fyodor Dostoevsky began one of the most revolutionary novels ever written, a work that marks the frontier, not only between nineteenth- and twentieth-century fiction, but between two centuries' visions of the self. For the unnamed narrator of *Notes from Underground* is a multiplicity of selves, each at war with the others—all at war with everything else.

Fiction/Literature

BY ANTON CHEKHOV

THE COMPLETE SHORT NOVELS

Chekhov, widely hailed master of the short story, also wrote five short novels. *The Steppe* is an account of a boy's frightening journey across the steppe of southern Russia. *The Duel* sets a fanatical rationalist and a man of literary sensibility on a collision course that ends in a series of surprising reversals. In *The Story of an Unknown Man*, a radical spying on an important official by serving as valet to his son gradually discovers that his terminal illness has changed his long-held priorities. *Three Years* recounts a complex series of ironies in the personal life of a rich but passive merchant. In *My Life*, a man renounces wealth for a life of manual labor. The resulting conflict between the moral simplicity of ideals and the complex realities of human nature culminates in an apocalyptic vision that is unique in Chekhov's work.

Fiction/Literature

BY NIKOLAI GOGOL

THE COLLECTED TALES OF NIKOLAI GOGOL

When Gogol left his Ukrainian village in 1828 to seek his fortune in St. Petersburg, he began composing marvelous stories—tales that combine the wide-eyed, credulous imagination of the peasant with the sardonic social criticism of the city-dweller. From the demon-haunted "St. John's Eve" to the strange surrealism of "The Nose," from the heartrending trials of the copyist in "The Overcoat" to those of the delusional clerk in "The Diary of a Madman," these stories allow readers to experience anew the unmistakable genius of a writer who paved the way for Dostoevsky and Kafka.

Fiction/Literature

DEAD SOULS

Since its publication in 1842, *Dead Souls* has been celebrated as a supremely realistic portrait of provincial Russian life and as a splendidly exaggerated tale; as a paean to the Russian spirit and as a remorseless satire of imperial Russian venality, vulgarity, and pomp. As Gogol's wily antihero, Chichikov, combs the back country wheeling and dealing for "dead souls"—deceased serfs who still represent money to anyone sharp enough to trade in them—we are introduced to a Dickensian cast of peasants, landowners, and conniving petty officials, few of whom can resist the seductive illogic of Chichikov's proposition. This lively, idiomatic English version by the award-winning translators Richard Pevear and Larissa Volokhonsky makes accessible the full extent of the novel's lyricism, sulphurous humor, and delight in human oddity and error.

Fiction/Literature